GRANDMA TALES

Edited by Lalita Iyer

Illustrations by
Vidya Gopal

SCHOLASTIC
New York Toronto London Auckland
Sydney New Delhi Hong Kong

Published by Scholastic India Pvt. Ltd.
A subsidiary of Scholastic Inc., New York, 10012 (USA).
Publishers since 1920, with international operations in Canada, Australia, New Zealand, the United Kingdom, India, and Hong Kong.

For information regarding permission, write to:
Scholastic India Pvt. Ltd.
A-27, Ground Floor, Sigma Centre
Infocity-1, Sector 34, Gurgaon 122001 (India)

First edition : August 2017
This reprint edition : February 2026

ISBN-13: 978-93-5275-165-5

Printed in India at Saurabh Printers Pvt. Ltd.

EDITOR'S NOTE

I am quite sure, like many of her kind all over the world, my mother is chuffed about her grandmother status. She was the first person to hold my son Re in her arms when he was born; she is always the first to wish him on his birthday and on every other occasion (and she never runs out of them). She is now also the one he meets when he gets back home from school, the only one he will discuss homework with, or take instructions on grooming from. On his part, he will remind his grandmother about taking her medicines or "not watching shouty channels", because "she has a new heart and has to look after it." (Re was four when my mother had her second valve replacement surgery.)

I sigh and let them be. I want Re to make the most of it now, as I know he doesn't have too many grandparent years left; two of his grandparents are in their eighties and two in their seventies already. He is at the leading edge of a generation whose mothers and fathers had children late in life. (TIME magazine calls it the grandparent deficit.)

I had both my grandmothers until my twenties; I don't know if my son will be that lucky.

When I compiled a few stories about my family for my earlier book, *The Boy who Swallowed a Nail and Other Stories*, I badly wanted to include a few of the stories Ammini (my grandmother) told me. I tried asking every member in the family tree to fill in the details that were missing, but it was in vain. All I could remember was her fart story (it was the best, so I was thankful). But I so wish I had written her stories (and so much else) down!

I reached out to the world and asked people to share stories about their grandmothers, stories their grandmothers told them. Some offered poems and recipes; others shared retellings of classics with the grandma garnish. In these retellings, essays, anecdotes and memories, there is a pickling of grandmas of sorts. There is, for instance, the nostalgia for a home and a matriarch that meant rootedness for every member of a family. There is a sense of awe for a steely grandmother who crushed a cobra to death and went about her chores, even as the men of the house gaped in horror. There's fond memories of food of a childhood that is characterised by laden tables (of different grandmothers). There are anecdotes of aspiring gossip columnist grandmas who secretly wanted their granddaughters to marry a Bollywood superstar and a little girl's visual memory of her grandaunt's mango pickle.

There are stories of friendship, memories of a dear friend left behind during partition, of cloth birds shaped from scraps of cloth by a grandmother who never wasted anything, of a wanderlusty grandchild who travelled the world with her grandma in a rucksack, and finally, grandmothers who were always thissing and thatting and you knew exactly what they meant.

I hope you see your grandmothers in some of these stories and that they will prompt you to go looking for stories of your own. Do share them with me at grandmatales@gmail.com

Don't worry, grandpas will follow soon. And that's a whole new book.

Lalita Iyer

CONTENTS

WHERE SWINGS COULD FLY

Andaleeb Wajid

There's a small swing set at the back of our house and it was our pride and joy when we were kids. We didn't have to go to the park to sit on the swing and pretend we could fly—we could do it right here at home! My father had ensured that it was an enclosed and private space so we could play on the swing as much as we liked. It was a proper swing set, not those creaky sofa set type thingies, and my brother and I would take turns at flying. Or so it seemed.

My parents went for Hajj every year, and my brother and I stayed back at home with my grandparents, aunt and uncle for company. While normally, spending time with my most favourite people should have pleased me, I couldn't fathom the idea of not seeing my mother for so long. I was used to long absences from my father who travelled abroad for business, but my mother was always there.

Nevertheless, my aunt who loved baking would lift us out of our blue moods with her food, while my grandmother, amma, would sit down with us in the evenings, in the backyard that had the swing set, and tell us stories. Some of my favourite, lazy afternoon memories, untouched by the pain of becoming an adolescent or teenager, were those simple quiet moments where either my brother or I were swinging lightly, while amma would put a mat on the ground, spread out all her crochet things before her. She would adjust her glasses and then, rocking very slowly, would relate to us stories that she remembered reading from old Urdu books.

What I remember most about those days was the undiluted joy of those moments when my brother and I would finish our homework and drag amma to the back of the house. Sometimes she told us stories from *Chidiyon ki Alif Laila.* Although I remember nothing of the stories now, it was the perfect beauty of that time that is seared into my mind. At other times she would recount to us stories of her pampered childhood, of how she and her sisters would go to school, how maids would bring them sumptuous lunches and all their classmates would vie with each other to get a taste of the yummy *shami kebab*s[1] that had been sent for them.

I think I imbibed my love of the past from her. It certainly played a huge role when I wanted to write

---

[1] a small patty of minced meat with ground chickpeas, egg to hold it together, and spices, cooked in the Indian sub-continent

a section of a story set in 1960 in my book *More than Just Biryani.* It was only when I was actually writing the story that I realised how acutely I missed amma. I wished I'd paid attention to her when she used to tell us stories of the old days, when there were no telephones, when they used to travel to each other's houses in cycle rickshaws or bullock carts (fully covered on all sides to ensure no one would get to sneak a look). She would relate to me stories of their mansion in Madras (not Chennai) and tell us of the cars they had, the movies they'd go and see (preferably Dilip Kumar's) in cinema halls, the thick slabs of Dairy Milk chocolate they'd eat, the train journeys they would take to Bangalore and the food that would be packed for them to eat on the way. But as I grew up, I had less and less patience for her stories.

I was caught up in my own world—studies, exams, marriage suddenly thrust upon me when I was only nineteen—but through it all, amma was there, looking at me with that constantly amazed expression on her face, like she couldn't believe

I was real. Her affection for me was so genuine, I never once doubted it or even thought about it. Then my son was born and she became a great-grandmother, a feat that was even more amazing for her, thanks to which I had snagged all brownie points from the other grandkids, for what would be forever.

She'd play with my son, tickle his feet as they waved in the air, continue to crochet her *namaz topi*s[2] while he played by her side and waited for the day when he would start walking, because she'd dreamt that he would come running to her when she called him. But she passed away, all too soon, suddenly, without any warning, when he was only nine months old.

I ache for him and the kids who came after him, for not knowing a grandmother like her who would tell them stories or simply just listen to them as they recounted a day in school. For secretly giving us big lumps of *amchur*[3] when our mother's

---

[2] skull cap for prayer

[3] mango powder

back was turned, or yelling at us with affectionate exasperation when we made too much noise.

The swing set at the back of my house is still there. My brother's kids and mine sometimes go there and swing away on it, unaware that a couple of decades ago, my brother and I used to be in their place, listening to stories of a Scheherazade-like bird and fairies and white elephants. I recently managed to find five of the *Chidiyon ki Alif Laila* Urdu books, and my son and I finished one book together, me reading Urdu painstakingly and my son puzzling over several words we never come across in our daily use of the language. I've considered taking these books to the place where magic used to happen, tell these stories to the kids, and although they have little patience or are too smart alecky, they do love to play on the swing. So maybe I will.

My grandmother's love for crochet and stories and our swing set where these stories would unfold forms the crux of this story.

MINTS AND MARBLES

Anjali Nayar

As soon as it turned four in the afternoon, I picked up my ball and ran out of the house. Yellow leaves had fallen on the road and they went *crunch-crunch* as I ran. The wind was crispy cold and the sky was so blue.

I ran to the giant red tree. Aditi was waiting there. We ran to the swings. I jumped on the yellow swing and Aditi sat on the green one. There was a jet flying in the sky. It was a tiny dot against a big, fluffy cloud, but it left a trail of smoke behind.

'Look!' I said, pointing up.

Aditi began to jump up and down. 'Byeeee bye,' she screamed, waving at the jet.

I laughed.

'I'll be going to Kerala!' Aditi said.

'What?' I replied.

'I'm making a photo album for my grandmother,' she was saying. 'Do you think she'll like it? And Mummy said I can pack my own suitcase this time!'

'But why?'

'I'm going to go to meet my grandparents, stupid! You forgot?'

I had a sinking feeling in my stomach as I remembered that summer was coming and it would be time for Aditi to go away for a whole month. 'When?' I whined, sticking my hands into my pockets and kicking at the mud. I suddenly didn't feel like playing anymore.

'Hey, look what I've got for you,' she said, trying to cheer me up. She took out two toffees from her pocket and gave me one. I grumpily tore off the wrapping and popped it into my mouth. It was mint. My favourite.

'Come on, smile,' she teased, pinching her cheeks wide and making googly eyes. It made me giggle. I always burst out laughing when Aditi did that.

***

But when I got home later, I didn't feel like eating my dinner or talking to anybody. I just sat by the window, staring at the sky as it went from orange to blue to black. Then I saw some movement in the reflection and felt a gentle touch on my head. I turned around to see my grandmother looking at me. 'What happened, beta?'

'Oh Dadi,' I blurted out, throwing my hands around her and burying my head into her shawl. 'Aditi will be leaving soon.'

'But that's a whole month away! Why be gloomy already?'

'But she's my best friend in the whole world, Dadi!' I scolded. 'You don't understand …'

'I know she's your best buddy, sweet girl …' she said, patting my shoulder. 'Say! Do you want to help me clean the sparrow-hut?'

'OK,' I agreed, following her into the veranda where she had hung a clay birdhouse. Every morning, she put some *roti* in it. And sparrows and squirrels came to eat it. She now took a paintbrush and dusted the birdhouse with it, peering into the tiny doors and windows through her wonky spectacles. She had taped her spectacles together with lots of sellotape so they wouldn't fall apart. A few days ago, when we were having dinner, one of her lenses popped out and rolled along the table. It clattered against Papa's plate and made me laugh so much that I choked on my food and Mummy had to get me water to feel better.

'We really need to get you new spectacles,' Papa insisted. 'You keep putting it off!'

‘Nah,’ Dadi dismissed the idea with a wave of her hand. ‘These are still good.’ She never *ever* threw anything out—I secretly thought she had saved everything she had owned since the beginning of time. Her rubber slippers were so worn, they had become like thin rubber wafers. And her glasses without the one lens sat wonky on her nose, but that didn’t prevent her from reading all three newspapers we got, from top to bottom and then the other way round.

She was always reading, my Dadi. She read all the storybooks I got from my library, and all the comic books and the picture books. Every day she climbed a chair to look into the sparrow’s nest to check if any new eggs had come. And sometimes she told me the strangest stories about fires and riots. Dadi wasn’t born in India, but in a little village really far away in Pakistan. She had lived there when she was a little girl until the fires swallowed the houses.

How it happened was that Dadi’s family was sleeping one night when she suddenly woke up.

There was a lot of shouting. 'I ran out to see what was going on,' Dadi told me, 'when I saw a huge orange blaze tearing towards me. All the huts were on fire!'

I gasped every time I heard about the huts on fire, and clutched her shawl.

'The villagers were running everywhere,' Dadi continued, staring into space as though she could still see the fires. 'They were screaming, "Run, run, they're coming to kill us!" Everyone was carrying their babies and running away. They all looked so frightened …'

'Then what did you do?'

'We also began running. We ran and ran until we had left the village behind and joined a huge queue of people making their way towards India. We couldn't take our calf; we couldn't take anything. Like us, everyone had come away with nothing. We had no food. There were thousands and thousands of us and we walked for days and days, I don't even know how many. All I remember is we were hungry and tired and frightened. When we finally reached Delhi, we found a place to stay, in a refugee camp. Later I was married to your grandfather.'

'Didn't you go back?'

'How could I, my dear?' she replied softly. 'My village has become Pakistan now.'

'Do you write to your friends?'

'Go and play now,' Dadi said. 'Look how beautiful it is outside—and the spring won't last forever.'

***

Outside, the trees were changing colour, and the winds began to get warmer. The sun blazed in the sky all afternoon. A few days after Aditi had told me that she was going to go to Kerala, I showed her my new marbles.

'These marbles have little fish in them!' she screamed. 'Oh, they are so pretty! Can I keep some?'

'No!' I grabbed the marbles back. 'Dadi gave them to me.'

Aditi looked so crestfallen that I regretted snatching the marbles away. I quickly gave the jar

back, saying, 'You can play with them as long as you want.'

'Fine,' she said grumpily, but she took the jar from my hands and spilled the marbles onto the grass. The sunlight fell on them, making them sparkle like stars. We lay in the grass, admiring how pretty they looked. The light was brightest in their centre. Little circles of light fell on the ground, following the marbles as we rolled them around with our fingertips.

Soon the days became hotter, and the grass dried up in the gardens. Crows hopped about with their open beaks, thirsty for water. So my Dadi set out an earthen pot filled with water for the sparrows, mynas, crows and squirrels. Even the ants came to drink the water. I know because I saw many dead ones floating in the pot.

The date for Aditi's departure was approaching, and our schools shut down for the vacations. Now I could spend all day playing, which made my mother anxious. 'Play only in the shade, *beta,*' she would call out from the house. 'Don't go running around in the sun, or you'll become red like a tomato.'

'Red tomato, red tomato, red tomato,' I sang, running down the road towards the park. The red tree had become brown and most of its leaves had fallen.

***

One evening I thought it would be fun to go cycling, so I called up Aditi to ask her, 'Should we go cycling today?'

'I can't come out today,' she answered regretfully. 'Mummy has said I have to finish my homework because we'll be going to Kerala soon.'

'But you can do it later,' I protested. 'And we can play something else if you don't want to go cycling.'

'I can't,' she replied sadly. 'I already had a fight with Mummy about it, and she's angry.'

'Will you come later?'

'I don't think so. She has banned me from going out.'

Feeling disappointed, I took my cycle out by myself. The other kids were playing together in the park and I tried not to stare at them. I went to the market road and cycled in squiggly patterns around the white road markers. Sometimes I pedalled super fast so I could go speeding downhill, stretching my legs out like a bird.

Then I saw something that almost made me lose my balance. Just as I was circling around Khajoor Park, I spotted Aditi coming down the road with another girl. They were clutching badminton rackets. I felt myself take in a sharp breath. Aditi and the other girl were closer now. I saw it was her cousin Nidhi. That's when Aditi noticed me and the smile disappeared from her face. I felt a sharp pain go through the centre of my chest and I whirled around and pedalled away furiously.

When I got home I slammed the door shut and ran into the bathroom. Everything got blurry as the tears began to pour out. When the phone rang, I hoped it wasn't Aditi, but Dadi called out to say, '*Beta*, it's Aditi on the line.'

Reluctantly I went and took the phone from Dadi's hands, who gave me a curious look before retreating into the kitchen.

'Hi,' Aditi said softly from the other side. 'I—I wanted to ask you—what time should we meet tomorrow to play?'

'I don't want to play with you tomorrow! You lied to me!'

'No! Nidhi and her mom came home without informing us; we didn't know they were going to come today. I swear!'

'Then when you saw me why didn't you ask me to join you?'

'But you cycled away so fast!'

'You're lying again!' I screamed, slamming down the phone.

I ran into the bathroom and burst into tears again. For the next few days, I didn't go out to play, nor did I call Aditi. And she didn't call me either. I tried to ignore the kids playing in the park, running around with their badminton rackets or cricket bats. I didn't talk to anyone, instead, stayed indoors, watching stupid TV shows I didn't even like.

***

One evening, Dadi asked me if I would walk with her to the tailor's shop to help her carry back some clothes. 'OK,' I said moodily. The evening air was nice, and there were blue and yellow butterflies flittering among the trees.

'If we cut through this park, we'll get there faster,' I told Dadi, leading her through the grass.

'Oh, look!' she exclaimed, stopping abruptly before a row of brightly-coloured pansies. She bent down to study the flowers, and suddenly burst into giggles.

'What are you laughing about?' I asked, startled.

'When I was a little girl,' she replied, 'I had a dear friend. She used to say that pansies looked like puppies.'

'Haha! No way,' I said.

Dadi turned a pansy towards me. 'Look at it. Doesn't it look like a dog's face?'

My eyes grew wide. 'Oh yes,' I said, giggling. 'It does look like a puppy!'

But as Dadi straightened back up, I saw the smile had disappeared from her face. 'Her name—

my friend's name—was Ruk … Ruk …' Dadi's voice quivered, choking. When she finally managed to say the name, it came out all crumpled, like she had buried it within herself for far too long.

'Rukhsana.'

I watched her quietly as she stared into the distance. 'One day, Rukhsana and I had a fight. I don't even remember now what it was about … But I got so mad at her that I just left from school without her. The next day Rukhsana didn't come to school. I don't know why. And that's the night the fires started in our village and we had to run.' Dadi took a deep breath. 'I never saw her again.'

My throat was beginning to hurt from holding back tears.

'Rukhsana stayed back in the village because she was Muslim. And we Hindus ran to India. And of course … I *never* got to see her again.' Her voice shook. 'It's been so long but I still think of her every day. And I wonder, what does she look like now? Does she also have a beautiful granddaughter like I do?'

I took Dadi's hand. Tears came into my eyes, but her face remained like steel. She picked out a blue pansy and put it in my hair. 'Blue was her favourite colour,' Dadi whispered.

Blue is Aditi's favourite colour also, I thought to myself painfully. The burning in my throat got worse.

Dadi and I walked home hand in hand, but I couldn't speak the entire way. That night, I climbed onto the water tank on our roof to watch the stars in the sky for a long, long time.

***

I couldn't sleep much at night, and kept tossing and turning in bed. But before the morning came, I was up and dressed. I heard the newspaper boy throw the newspapers into our house. Then I quietly opened the front door and went out to wait by the gate. A sweeper was cleaning the street, and a milkman was delivering milk packets to the doorsteps. The sky became brighter. Vegetable and fruit sellers began coming by with their carts.

There was honking as a taxi pulled up in front of Aditi's house, and the driver got out to ring the doorbell. Aditi's father came out with two big suitcases and put them into the taxi. Next, her mother came out with the baby, saying, 'Have we got everything?'

At last, Aditi come out through the door, wearing a Minnie Mouse T-shirt and holding a little pink suitcase. On seeing me, she froze in the doorway, staring silently. I took a deep breath and began to walk towards her. My heart hammered in my chest. I felt terrified at her blank expression but I tried to be brave. There was a small bundle in my hands. I took her hand and pressed the bundle into it.

She looked at me quizzically. 'Open it,' I whispered. She put down her bag and unknotted the handkerchief. Green marbles with fish in their bellies winked in the sunlight. Aditi looked up at me with big questioning eyes.

'These are yours,' I said. 'Half of mine.'

Aditi's lip began to tremble as she looked down at the marbles. When she looked back up at me, I saw she had tears in her eyes.

'Hurry up, Aditi!' her mother was calling. 'We'll miss our train!'

Aditi clutched the marbles in her fist and turned away from me to follow her mother to the taxi. She stood by the boot as the driver put her suitcase in the car. She wasn't even looking at me anymore, and I felt the pain grow sharp in my chest. 'Come on,' Aditi's mother urged her. Aditi raised her foot to climb in, then stopped to look back at me.

I quickly looked down. Everything was getting blurry again. Suddenly, I saw two bunny shoes walk into my view, and I looked up at Aditi in surprise. She was smiling a little. 'Next month,' she whispered mischievously, 'I'll beat you with my new magic marbles.'

I stared at her, blinking, and exploded into laughter so suddenly that tears spilled down my cheeks. Aditi jumped and threw her arms around me. Her hair flew into my face and tickled my nose, but I didn't mind. Then I felt her put something into my pocket before she pulled back and ran towards the waiting taxi.

I watched as she got into the car. The exhaust pipe let out a puff of smoke and then the taxi lurched into the street. Aditi leaned out of the window, waving at me frantically. 'I'll miss you ...' she yelled. The next thing I knew, the taxi had disappeared down the road in a swirl of dust, carrying away my best friend.

I waved, sighing deeply. Then I turned around and began to walk sadly back home. That's when I felt the lump in my pocket. I slipped it out and looked at it.

It was my favourite mint candy, wrapped in a handkerchief.

'Come back soon, Aditi!' I whispered to the empty road. 'Come back soon, my best friend!'

The character of the grandmother in my story is inspired by my grandmother, who migrated to India with her family during the partition in 1947. She missed her home but she couldn't go back. One of her deepest regrets was that she forgot to carry her college certificates when she escaped. But she loved to read and learn, and she continued to study on her own. She was fluent in Punjabi, Hindi, English and Urdu, and she always watched the Urdu news in order to keep up her practice. She was brave, feisty and intelligent. She died when she was 87 years old, and ever since then I've missed her a lot. But someday, I hope I can go find the village she grew up in and find my roots.

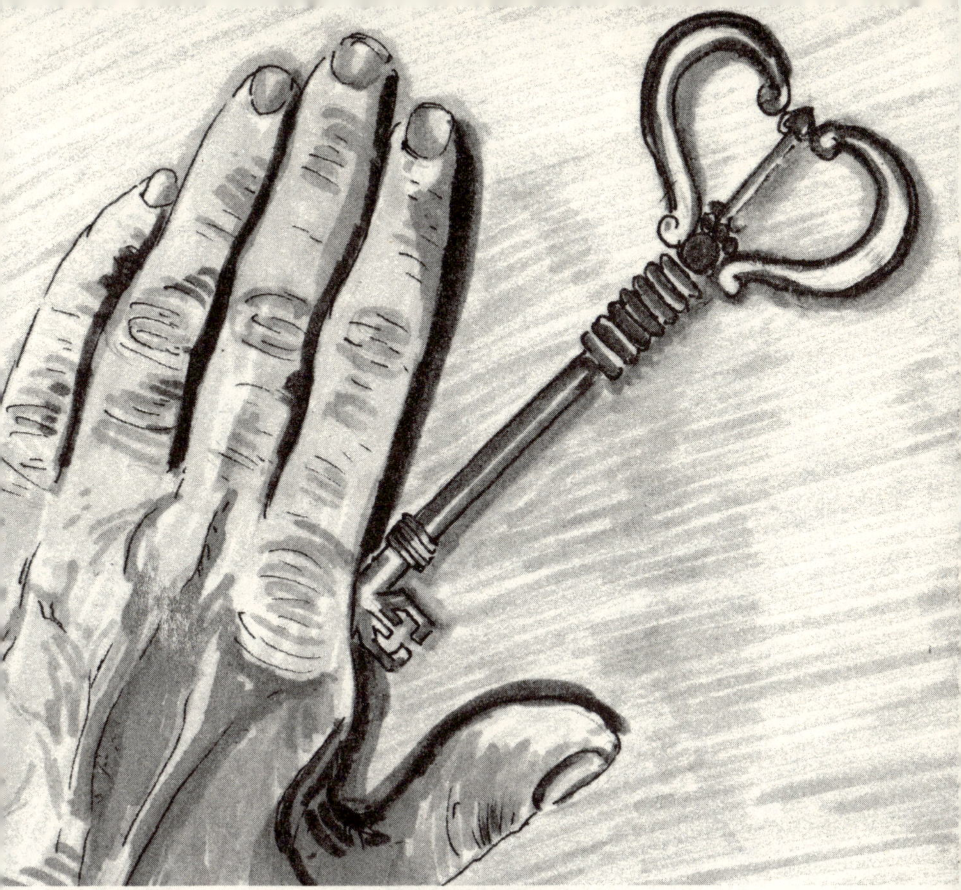

HEIRLOOM

Arundhathi Subramaniam

My grandmother,
wise even at eight,
hid under her bed
when her first suitor came home.

Grave and serene
her features, defined
as majestically as a head
on an old coin, I realise
through photographs, clouded
by the silt of seasons, like the patina
of age on Kanjeevaram silks,
that in her day, girls of eight didn't
have broken teeth or grazed elbows.

Now in her kitchen,
she quietly stirs ancestral
aromas of warm coconut lullabies,
her voice tracing the familiar
mosaic of family fables, chipped
by repetition.

And yet,
in the languorous swirl
of sari, she carries the secret
of a world where nayikas still walk
with the liquid tread of those
who know their bodies as well
as they know their minds, still glide

down deserted streets—to meet
dark forbidden paramours whose eyes
smoulder like lanterns in winter—
and return before sunset, the flowers
in their hair radiating the perfume
of an unrecorded language of romance.

The secret of a world
that she refuses to bequeath
with her recipes
and her genes.

(From *Where I Live: New and Selected Poems*; Bloodaxe Books, UK, 2009.)

It is often difficult to believe grandparents were ever young—much less to imagine they might have once had a romantic life. This is a somewhat baroque recreation of my grandmother's early amorous career. But it is also a yearning for the sense of self-possession she exuded.

GAGRU AND GAGRI

Aryaman Khandelwal

After suiting up for work, Gagru smiled at Gagri, who was helping him knot his tie. 'Prepare some hot supper for the evening. Today I will not be long. We will eat our supper and we can go to the mall to shop for my beautiful wife,' he said. Gagru himself was quite a romantic, but today Gagri noticed a certain sparkle in his eyes. It made her feel special. Gagru held a very high financial position in an important multinational insurance company, and as a result, this couple seldom spent a night on a date. Gagri was ecstatic to finally be able to get out of her home with her husband. She bid him goodbye and Gagru left the house for work.

After finishing the household chores, Gagri wore her best outfit and left the house to buy ingredients for supper. Within a couple of hours, all her raw materials were in place, and she headed back home to cook them. After a satisfying lunch, she began cooking supper. In India, for supper, a traditional family sometimes eats a *khichri*, which is a recipe using rice, pulses and turmeric. The couple loved this dish, although some people might find it bland. She put the rice into the pan and started the fire on the stove. A few minutes later, she added

the pulses, and soon after, she put the turmeric. Whilst she waited for the khichri to cook, she started making tea, which was a regular evening drink for any couple. In an hour, Gagri was excited to see the supper ready. She decided to taste the khichri to ensure that all the flavours were right. She picked up a spoon from the drawer and had a spoonful of the dish. It was delicious. Truly, it was perhaps the best khichri she had cooked in a long time. Looking at the piece of art, she thought to herself, 'Well, one more bite can never hurt.' She took another bite, and another one, and another. Before she knew it, the khichri was over. Only the burnt rice on the bottom was left. 'I'll cook some more up. It won't take more than half an hour,' she told herself.

Opening her cabinet, Gagri panicked for a minute when she realised that she had run out of rice. Her face turned pale, and she sat on the couch, crying. 'I ruined our supper. It was so selfish of me.' After half an hour of sobbing, she was very tired. Slowly, she fell asleep.

After an hour or so, she heard the front door creek open, and from the corner of her eye, she saw Gagru walk in. 'Hello dear,' he said, 'I hope the supper is ready. I cannot wait for some hot khichri and tea. I'll take a quick shower. Then we can have supper and head to the mall.' Gagri was too sleepy to reply. She simply nodded her head. Fifteen minutes later, Gagru came out of the shower and headed to the kitchen. 'Darling, where is it?' he asked.

'Look under the plates,' she replied.

Gagru looked, and found nothing. He shouted, 'Darling, where is the khichri?'

'Look under the stove,' he heard.

He looked under the stove, to find nothing. Slightly irritated this time, he repeated, 'Darling, where is it?'

'Look in the glasses,' Gagri said in a rather groggy voice.

Gagru looked in the glasses, and once again found nothing. 'Darling, where is it? he sounded a bit angry.

Gagri called out, 'Look in the pan,' whilst walking to the kitchen. Gagru looked in the pan, and found burnt rice under the khichri. He was furious. Gagri came into the kitchen. Gagru picked up the burnt rice, and threw it at Gagri's face. 'What is this? I thought you had cooked supper. Is this it?'

Gagri's ear was injured. The intense heat of the rice had burnt it. 'What have you done, Gagru? I was going to apologise,' she cried. She picked up her phone and money, and dashed out of the house before any further violence.

She headed to the goldsmith to exchange her jewellery for some cash for the doctor and chemist. 'Listen, goldsmith, give me some money in exchange of this gold jewellery. After that, I will go to my mother.'

After receiving some money, she went to the doctor to get herself treated. 'Listen, doctor, treat my injuries, and heal me. After that I will go to my mother. The doctor took a look at her patient and prescribed some medicines.

Then she headed to the chemist. 'Listen, chemist, give me these medicines. Then I will go to my mother.'

The chemist looked at the prescription and provided Gagri with the medicines. She paid him the money, and headed to her mother's place.

Her mother was rather surprised to see her daughter comc home at this time. 'What happened, my child? How come you are here? Is everything alright?' she asked.

Gagri could not help her tears, and she told her mother the entire story as accurately as she could. 'Oh, that's terrible, dear! Both of you did wrong. You were wrong in eating his share of the supper, but he should not have reacted so violently.' I will cook up some khichri now, and call Gagru over.

Whilst Gagri treated her wounds, her mother summoned Gagru, sending him a message. 'I heard about today, child. I do not blame you. Both of you should learn looking beyond each other's mistakes. There are so many good qualities in the two of you. Focus on them. Forgive my daughter.

Come here. I have cooked some khichri. You two can eat that and head home.'

Half an hour later, Gagru came to his mother-in-law's house. She served the couple her handmade khichri, which was popular among the common folk for its delicious taste. Both Gagru and Gagri enjoyed their supper.

'I'm sorry, dear. I should not have reacted the way I did. Can you forgive me?' Gagru asked Gagri.

Gagri replied, 'Of course, darling. And I am sorry for eating your share of the khichri. It was very selfish of me.'

'That's alright,' remarked Gagru. The couple joyfully went home, and enjoyed the rest of the day. Gagru and Gagri had a perfect evening, after all.

This story was a classic for my maternal grandmother (Nani), who was more of a mother to me than a grandmother. She raised me as her own child, and I cannot thank her enough. This piece is dedicated to you, Nani. Thank you for all you did for me.

As a child, this story would always be a go-to, whether to make me finish lunch or to put me to bed. To be fair, I really enjoyed this story. She would recite this story to me in Kashmiri, adding her own twists to it over the years. Traditionally, in Kashmiri, gagru means a male mouse, while a gagri is a female mouse. In her version of the story, however, Gagru and Gagri are a man and a woman respectively. Perhaps she stuck with the names because the characters were close to her heart.

BAI

Avantika Agarwal

When I was a little girl, I used to spend all my school holidays in Jodhpur. My Dad grew up there in a huge house with giant doors (that had scary brass spikes on them), with a lovely grill-covered courtyard in the middle of it, and upstairs, there was a double terrace that provided an uninhibited view of the majestic Mehrangarh fort.

In the summers, desert coolers would hum all day long and the only time we would not be sitting in front of the cool blast of air they threw at us was when it was time to refill them with water, one heavy bucket at a time. Afternoons would be spent making *laddoo*s out of mud and then baking them in the harsh sun until they were hard enough to be used as ammo in mock wars. Come evening, all of us cousins would run up to the terrace to sprinkle water on the hot roof to cool it down. And then we would roll out our individual mattresses and guard them with our lives so that nobody lay down on them and warmed them up before bedtime.

During the Diwali holidays, coolers would be replaced with fat *rajai*s[4] that were heavier than my youngest cousin! The house would be filled with yummy smells and sounds of *mathri*s[5] and

[4] quilt

[5] a flaky biscuit from north-west of India, mostly Rajasthan

shakarparas[6] being fried by the kilo, in the kitchen. My grandfather would bring out his collection of scratchy woollen caps to protect his bald pate, all the time trying to sneak in fried goodies from the kitchen to his room, and there would be a general air of festivity in the house for a good fortnight.

And in the background of all of this, going quietly about her day, taking all the important (and not-so-important) decisions, was my great-grandmother.

Bai, as she was called, was the quintessential busy bee. I don't ever remember her sitting idle. Even when she couldn't move around a lot in her old age, she insisted on helping around the house. So, if she wasn't helping my aunts in the kitchen, rolling out close to forty rotis every mealtime (with a speed and precision that boggled me), she was folding the giant pile of laundry that a joint family generates every other day. She would clean and chop veggies, sort and stack utensils, even wash and dry her own clothes.

---

[6] western Indian snack, mostly made in Gujarat and Maharashtra, made from a dough of milk, sugar, ghee, maida, semolina and salt

Bai belonged to a generation that lived differently. She often told us how lucky we were to have so many conveniences—most of which we took for granted—like running water and electricity. We would hear about how she had to walk several kilometres every day to get water, and each time the mixer-grinder would be switched on, she would reminisce about the stone grinder that was now catching dust in a dark corner of the house. I, for one, was glad because I had tried my hand at that stone grinder and I definitely didn't have the fitness levels required to grind even a handful of dal!

She was a patient soul, Bai. As little kids, my sister and I would spend hours playing with her super soft and wrinkly skin, pulling it in all directions, very amused by the elasticity. She even let us comb and braid her hair—the one thing she didn't know how to do on her own. Why? Because, traditionally, a *nayan*[7] would come home to wash, oil and braid her hair once a week and that's how it had been all her life. Of course, my hair braiding skills were average

[7] a barber's wife

at best and after indulging me as only a great-grandmother can, she would get one of my aunts to redo her hair so that she looked presentable!

And every once in a while, she would open the lock to a room that was once used as the winter bedroom by my great-grandparents. Behind the heavy, cream-coloured wooden doors was a room that was warm, and smelled of cashews and old *ittar*[8], and was a veritable treasure trove for us. Bai would rummage around in old metal boxes with fading designs and rusted handles and little drawstring *potli*s[9] made of red velvet, taking something out, putting other things in. Rajais with maroon velvet covers would be piled high along with old pillows and bolsters on a gorgeous wooden bed. And they made the perfect spot from which to jump and land in a higgledy-piggledy pile on the floor, laughing uncontrollably.

Outside this room was a diwan on which Bai would take her afternoon naps and repose for the night. Under her pillow lay her bunch of keys. It

[8] an essential oil distilled with water to make a natural perfume
[9] packets

was here that she rested between her multitude of chores, usually accompanied by my grandfather, and very often with a sewing basket and a large pile of random scraps of cloth.

No piece of cloth ever got thrown away. If it couldn't become a dusting cloth, it made its way to huge drawstring cloth bags under Bai's bed, put away for use at a later time. Collected over the years, I recognised my little cousin's frocks in several pieces of cotton cloth, with polka dots and flowery prints. There were pieces of cloth that looked like they belonged to the cushion covers in the living room. And then there were shiny, glittery, slightly gaudy pieces that Bai had used to make clothes out of for the idols in the temple at home.

These shiny scraps of cloth are my fondest memory of Bai.

What looked like a haphazard collection of kitschy material to me became works of art in Bai's hands. I remember asking her once why she collected these little snippets of cloth. And she sat me down and showed me. She started with dividing the cloth into pairs, and since there was never enough to have two of the same print or colour, it was fascinating to see how instinctively she put together patterns and colour combinations. Then, without even the suggestion of an inch tape or a ruler or a tailor's chalk, she cut all the cloth into equal-sized squares. Just like that. Next, tiny triangles were cut from plain-coloured cotton scraps and I still wasn't sure where this was going. I did help, though. My young eyes and hands were entrusted with threading the needle so that Bai could sew. And within minutes of her getting a needle, I knew what we were making—pretty little colourful birds for one of those hangings synonymous with Rajasthan.

Except that these birds had more character and charm than any commercially available string of birds did. These were handmade by Bai. Each piece of cloth carefully chosen and hand-stitched, little beaks and tails tacked on and then stuffed full of old scraps of cloth. Even today, those birds evoke the memory of me sitting under a squeaky fan one lazy afternoon with my great-grandmother, watching her make birds out of scrap material and being amazed at what she was creating even at her age.

That memory of hanging out with Bai and discovering that some of my creativity and love for craft was probably inherited from her is one of my fondest memories of my great-grandmother.

I feel lucky to have known Bai. To be able to say that my great-grandmother taught me something, or to quote one of her life lessons in a tricky situation, is fortunate indeed. And I can't wait till my son is old enough to learn how to make little cloth birds with me sitting him down and showing him how to do it. Just like Bai did with me.

"Bai" *is a story about the author's childhood vacations spent in Jodhpur. A story about her great-grandmother and the very special person she was.*

THE DAY MY GRANDMOTHER BECAME A GOSSIP COLUMNIST

Bijal Vachharajani

I think we can all agree that the standard job description for a grandparent is—spoiler of grandchildren, spinner of yarns, and provider of yummy bribes. Nowhere does it ever mention that one of your grandparents will also take it upon herself to become a gossip columnist, that too about one of their precious grandkids, who should ideally be the apple of their eye. Seriously, Grandma, there's only one journalist in this family, and that's me. And I do not write gossipy stories.

Okay, I am getting ahead of myself. Let's start from the beginning. There I was, in my first ever job, aspiring to be the best ever in whatever it was that I was doing. I worked for an animal rights organisation, and loved my job. I got to help animals, work with people who loved animals, and even shoot with celebrities who loved animals.

One of my biggest assignments was organising a shoot with a Bollywood actor. Our team was working 24x7 (that means pretty much all the time—24 hours in a day, seven days a week, you get the picture), piecing together every little aspect of this shoot. From costumes to set design, photography to film-making, everything had to be perfect. By the end of it, I was a nervous wreck—I don't think I had slept in days (or nights, for that matter), eaten a meal sitting down, and there was a distinct red mark on my ear from being glued to my Nokia cell phone like forever. Hey, film stars can be very demanding!

At last it was over. I was grateful that the shoot had gone well, but if I never saw another Bollywood film, it would be perfectly fine with me. I was kind of done with shoots. Of course, my team knew that, and in what they thought was a very clever move, gifted me a framed picture of the film actor and me standing together. Ha ha! Thanks, guys, that's all I needed, a reminder of a crazy few days!

I grudgingly took the photo frame home and tried to hide it under my mattress. Then I thought with horror that someone would think I liked him so much that I wanted to sleep with his picture under my pillow. So I was forced to remove the frame, and that's when my mother saw it. Like proud parents are known to do, she lovingly dusted the photo and gave it pride of position on our bookshelf in the living room, where no one—from guests to the ironing man to the cook—would miss it. I thought this was the worst it would get. Oh, how mistaken I was!

A few days later, I got a call from my uncle. He sounded concerned. 'Why didn't you tell us?' he asked, sounding hurt.

'Tell you what?' I asked, rifling through all that had happened over the last few days. Perhaps he had heard about the turtle rescue we did, and had suddenly developed an interest in amphibians.

'Arrey, you know, I really thought we would be the first ones to know,' he said.

Considering our turtle rescue had made it to the news, I couldn't understand how he had expected me to tell him before the press.

'You read it in the papers?' I asked.

'It's in *the papers*?' My uncle really sounded upset.

'Ummm … yes.'

'Why wouldn't you tell us that you're getting married?' he asked.

Wait, what! Where did that come from? Who was getting married?

'I am not getting married,' I said. 'Who told

you I am getting married? And why would it be in the papers? Huh!'

'Of course you are,' he said. 'Your Dadi came over yesterday and she said that your parents have chosen a boy for you, and you both are happily posing for a photo, and they have even framed and put it up in the living room.'

I honestly didn't know whether to laugh or cry. Really, Grandma! Letting her imagination run wild and marrying me off, and that too to a film star.

I ran back home, marched up to the bookshelf and took down the offending photo frame.

The next day, my grandmother asked me where the photo was. 'What photo?' I asked. 'There was no photo here, ever.' I scurried into my room, leaving a very puzzled-looking grandmother squinting at the empty space on the bookshelf.

A grandmother is pretty pleased when she discovers that her granddaughter is finally ready to settle down. Actually, not discovers, "thinks"! A story about getting your wires crossed, and how.

IT'S ALL IN THE GENES

Bijal Vachharajani

There she was, my sister, on top of a car. Not inside it. She was actually on top of it. She had scrambled onto the bonnet of the Ambassador car and then hauled herself onto its roof. All in a bid to get away from a yapping Pomeranian.

It's always been a puzzle in my family—there I was, rescuing animals from circuses and illegal traders, dropping off orphaned chickens and blind snakes to shelters, and feeding malnourished cats and dogs; while my sister would take off, running at an enviable speed, even at the sight of a tail or a hairy paw. She's been known to jump an entire flight of stairs while being chased by a dog (another Pomeranian), taken to her heels in front of a cow who obligingly broke into a trot and decided to give chase, and pointed a finger dramatically at a puppy and yelled, 'He's going to bite me, I know he is,' while said puppy looked on, puzzled.

I had clearly picked up this affinity for furry and feathered creatures from my Mum. Ever since I can remember, she was bringing quivering kittens home and coaxing them into health, feeding big fat strays who clearly didn't need more chapatis, and leaving seeds and water out for birds. My Mum had spent a good part of her childhood living on the outskirts of Bhuj in Gujarat, close to a forest. Owls knocking on their door, cobras curled up in their toilets and over-affectionate cows were all pretty commonplace for her.

My father, while not batty about animals, was fairly affable around them. He'd pat a kitten on its tiny head, or whistle at a rescued bird, or hover anxiously around an injured animal, until they'd left for their next destination. Which is why my sister's phobia was one of the greatest mysteries of the Vachharajani clan.

Years passed, and my Mum and I were chatting about her mother (my grandmother). I was barely six years old when she passed away, and if I squeeze my eyes shut and try to think of her, I can remember a wispy bespectacled figure with kind, twinkling eyes, always busy doing something. I don't even know if it's a real memory or something I stole from a black-and-white photograph. Perhaps it is a bit of both.

As Mum was reminiscing, stories spilled out, one over the other—of lullabies sung to me as a baby, heaps of food lovingly prepared during festivals, and family holidays and picnics taken together. I, of course, didn't remember anything. Then my Mum suddenly said, 'Do you remember the porch in our Delhi house?'

'Of course, the one with lots of plants,' I said. 'And your favourite jasmine pot.'

'Yes, your grandmother loved sitting there in the daytime, soaking in the winter sun,' she said, a smile in her voice. 'But she'd hate it when the cats came.'

'Cats?' I asked. 'You mean Jinglu-Minglu?' I remembered that pair, two plump white and yellow cats who'd come mewing for food everyday. They were quite wild, but would let my mother feed them and give them an occasional pat on the head. Also, all animals were named Jinglu-Minglu by my Mum, to keep it simple.

'Yes, yes,' she said. 'Jinglu-Minglu. Your grandmother was terrified of them.'

What! This was the first I had heard of this. 'Really?' I asked incredulously. 'She was scared of cats?'

'Oh yes, petrified. She'd see them and start yelling, 'Take them away! Take them away! They will bite me.' And the cats would look so puzzled.'

As she said that, we both fell silent and looked at each other. And collapsed into laughter. Finally we knew where my sister's fear of animals came from—our very own grandmother. Down to the finger-pointing and the dramatic yelling.

The fear of cats is called ailurophobia. And the author's family has a weird mix of people who love them and those who are terrified of them.

THE TRAVELLING AMMUMA

Arathi Menon

The day my grandmother died, her smile walked off her lips and into my heart.

My grandmother, or Ammuma as I called her,

was like a wren. Or a robin. She was a frail, chirrupy bird with bright intelligent eyes and a smile that never left her face. You would find her twittering around the kitchen, whipping up delicious meals. She even had a little bench there, where visitors would sit and yak away.

As a child, I would sometimes crawl under that bench and listen to the local gossip or an aunty complaining about her son who had thrown the cat into the well. If the tales were too long, Ammuma would secretly hand me a small bowl of jackfruit chips. I would nibble each chip silently so that I wouldn't disturb the complaining lady.

Every summer I would hop on a train to Kerala. When I reached our ancestral house, I would throw my knapsack on the muddy compound and rush to the kitchen to hug Ammuma. She was old-fashioned and would protest, 'Stop hugging me—that's what English people do.' I wouldn't listen. Over the years she learnt to hug me back.

Ammuma was born before we got our independence. She studied up to the sixth standard.

She had six children and a gazillion grandkids, amongst whom I was one. Though she hadn't been to college, she was the wisest person I had ever met. She knew what to apply to soothe a centipede bite, how to get rid of a hiccup, the best way to pluck a guava from a tree with a beehive, how to calm her enraged daughter (my mother) and which leaf to eat when you got a stomach cramp from gorging on too many mussels.

I have never seen her unhappy or crabby or moody. She is, perhaps, the only person in my life who has never gotten angry with me. The kitchen was her kingdom. Here she would hum songs I didn't know, and create unpronounceable but yummy things. From odd-coloured sweet drinks to spicy-salty mangoes to sticky jackfruit toffee. I just had to walk in and her hand would disappear into one of the large *bharani*s (jars) that were scattered around, to unearth a goody for a hungry face.

Two weeks after she passed away, I got a courier. Her eldest son, my uncle, had framed a photograph of her and sent it to the extended family. The picture measured six by six inches and held within it her smiling face and the kind eyes I loved so much. Like the Mona Lisa I was to see years later, her eyes always seemed to be shining at me.

The image was a simple black and white photo with a matt finish. However, through some magic of light, it had managed to capture the essence of her. When my mother and I saw it, we felt my Ammuma hadn't gone anywhere. She was still here with us.

I began taking the photo everywhere with me. Ammuma's first trip was to a rock climbing camp in Hampi, Karnataka. She travelled in my rucksack. There, after I scaled a fifty-feet monolithic rock, much to the amusement of my fellow climbers, I took her out and showed her the view. I think she liked it.

That was the beginning of her adventures. She happily came along on my fourteen-day road trip from Delhi to Leh and didn't get car-sick. She enjoyed one month in Kyrgyzstan and never complained about the food. She experienced the beautiful cold of Sydney, witnessed the fashion of Paris and got lost in the surreal landscape of the deserts of Dubai. For someone who had never left her village when she was alive, she was now a well-travelled Granny.

Whenever I moved cities, she moved with me. The first thing I would do when I entered my rented space in an alien town would be to take her out and place her in a convenient corner. The place would immediately stop feeling strange and unknown. Instead, it would turn cozy and familiar. Bengaluru, Mumbai, Kolkata, Delhi, Chennai, Dubai, Bahrain—she has seen quite a lot of living quarters, and with her presence made each one a sanctuary for me.

Once, a cousin of mine I hadn't met in ten years was faced with an emergency. He wanted to stay at my place for a night. I was travelling at that time and I asked him to take a spare key from a friend. The only problem was that my apartment complex had 160 identical flats. I cautioned him to be extra careful while reading the door number, for

nobody likes to be awakened at 3 a.m. by a stranger.

Armed with the key, he entered a house but was unsure whether it was my place. He told me he felt like a burglar and was petrified of getting caught. He switched on the light and the first thing that caught his eye was my Ammuma's photo. He broke into a smile … he had come to the right place. He had an identical picture in his house too.

I have often been asked to make her carry a small photograph of hers. Concerned well-wishers enquire whether the present one is too large, too bulky to carry around. They say it would be better for me to have something small, that I can tuck into my purse. I shake my head. I like the size of her photograph. Its chunkiness is reassuringly perfect.

For someone like me who's been a gypsy and has had to live in different places, with different furniture and friends every two years, my Ammuma has been the single steady constant in my life. I sometimes think of myself as a walking tree and her as my root. No matter where I go, when I decide to pause and set her down, I know I have come home.

THE UNSAFETY CATCH

Helen D'Souza

Train journeys always promise adventure. In the days when I was young, families lugged along many tin trunks with names and destinations painted on them, leather suitcases falling apart, but for the twine that held them together, and bundles of food that could feed half the compartment. There was a sending-off party that waited with the travellers, bringing even more bundles to carry to relatives far away. The train, when it finally rolled in, was greeted with feverish excitement, and coolies ran alongside, balancing bags like tiles on their heads.

Of course, this train trip would offer an adventure of quite another kind.

After a hot, hectic day at the Delhi Zoo, I was glad to relax on the berth of our first class coupe. It would be ours alone, and for those hours, our travelling home—food would be set out, and bedsheets spread. My feet were sore and I felt the throb of a dozen bongos in my poor aching head. My husband, our three-year-old daughter and I were returning to our home in Jamshedpur, a charming little city in Bihar. This being long before mobile phones and emails gave minute-to-minute coverage, we did not know what would greet us; floods and famines were common features.

'I must make the most of this journey and rest,' I said to my husband. 'Since I have a splitting headache, will you sleep on the lower berth—and I'll stretch out on the top with Baby?'

'Sure.' He locked the safety catch on the metal door of our private coupe with a resounding clang.

The train had now gained momentum, and with my days of athletics far behind me, coupled with the rocking of the train and my ample proportions, climbing to the top berth was a feat worth mentioning. However, with the aid of my groaning husband, I finally hoisted myself up, and then pulled our daughter up. Swallowing an aspirin, I lay down and was in dreamland within five minutes. Our little girl, exhausted after her exciting holiday in Delhi, fell asleep equally promptly, while my husband sat up reading.

It was a sultry night, and the windows were open, letting the dark countryside flash by, punctuated by a few lit posts or stations. It was one in the morning when my husband decided to turn in, he later told me, and by two, he was shaking the rafters with his snores.

It couldn't have been more than a few minutes later when his eyes flicked open, by instinct, sixth sense or what have you. Directly in his line of vision was a large, burly man clad in khaki or murky green—it was dark, and difficult to really make out. He had a bag slung across him, and seemed to be struggling with the door.

'What do you want?' my husband called out.

The man muttered, 'I'm the ticket collector, but you go back to sleep. And shut the door, shut the door. You should be careful.'

Sleepily, my husband padded to the door as the ticket collector moved away down the rocking corridor, and pulled the door shut once more, automatically reaching for the safety catch.

'Hullo,' he thought. 'I'm positive I had fastened this safety catch before retiring. How did the ticket collector open the door?' The thought snapped him awake. He beetled his bushy eyebrows in puzzlement.

He stepped outside, looking to the left and right, down the darkened corridor with only silhouettes of passengers asleep under their blankets. Deciding

to explore the situation at that hour of the night, (he'd read too many detective novels, for sure), he walked along the corridor of the coach. There was no ticket collector, not even the usual carriage attendant. Instead, one of the coach doors hung open, swaying with the rock and roll of the train.

Our friendly ticket collector seemed to have departed with supersonic suddenness.

My husband returned to our coupe, and when the train drew up at the next station, he hailed a passing policeman to report the strange case. It was only then that I finally awoke and asked what the ruckus was all about. The policeman examined the door and agreed it was a forced entry; he even pointed out the missing bulbs in the train (never mind the missing attendant).

'Go back to sleep,' my husband told me. 'It was only a thief entering our coupe.'

'What?' I sat up instantly, of course. 'How—when—good heavens!'

'See this half-inch gap between the door and its frame?' my husband pointed it out. 'Quite sufficient to insert a wire and lift the safety latch off its cradle. Our visitor did just that. Here, the wire marks are visible.'

'Thank goodness he didn't decamp with anything, or any of us,' I said, relieved. After a moment's pause, a new thought made its entry into my easily anxious mind. 'He may return.'

'That's a possibility.'

We both sat plotting ways to keep the intruder from staging a repeat performance. With no ticket collector, attendant or policeman now on call, it was turning slightly menacing. After moments of concentrated thinking, my husband piped up, 'I have a brilliant idea.' By his tone and the gleam in his eyes, you would think he'd won the State Lottery.

'What is it? Tell me, tell me.' But he was rummaging in our suitcase, allowing me to simmer with curiosity.

Those were the days when we travelled with almost our entire possessions, in case of an emergency. As he fished out a metal shirt hanger, his brilliant dark eyes lit up.

‘Are you going to use that as a weapon?’ I made a wild guess, and in my fertile imagination, I conjured up pictures of my brave husband, like the knights of old, fencing with the faceless thief and brandishing a—*shirt hanger*!

‘Just watch me,’ said my hero, and as I watched, perplexed, he bent and twisted the hanger around the safety catch. ‘I’ve made the unsafety catch safe once more,’ he wise-cracked, and appeared to be waiting for applause.

‘You’re a genius,’ I said.

‘So now let’s turn off the lights and return to our slumber,’ he quipped happily.

With the lights off once more, and no sleep approaching, I called down, ‘Are you awake?’ Deep sonorous breathing was my only answer. I closed my eyes and tried sleeping desperately. After all, I was the one who needed rest; I was the one with the headache. But the slightest sound drew my eyes to the door.

In my feverish condition, I imagined scenarios of thieves plunging knives into our bellies, and on occasion, even wondered if it were a ghost. Angrily, I shook off my silly worries and as I peeped once more at that safety catch, my tired eyes actually saw it heaving upwards again—like a seesaw, up and down.

Finally, I threw in the towel, and sat up with my eyes glued to the safety catch all night long, for although I admired the ingenuity of my husband, I did not for a moment underestimate our marauder. I pulled out the remaining metal shirt hanger and held it ready, much like the knight myself.

I vowed this would be a story I'd tell my grandchildren. And right here, right now, that's exactly what I'm doing.

Helen D'Souza had a lifetime of story-telling, first as a kindergarten teacher and piano teacher in Jamshedpur, and then as a primary school principal. The wondrous tales from her past continued as bedtime stories for her grandsons. This story, told to her author daughter Jane D'Souza, is her last story, as she passed away soon after its telling.

THISSING AND THATTING

Jerry Pinto

Now the trick thing about grannies is that everyone gets two. The trickier thing about great-grandmothers is that everyone gets four. The trickier still thing about great-great-grandmothers is that everyone gets sixteen. After that, I get dizzy and have to sit down, so you can figure out how many great-great-great-great-great-great grandmothers you have. I have a story to tell here and all this mathematics is distracting me.

The reason I mention this is because I had a Byculla Granny and a Goa Granny. I also had a Mahim Granny and a Nagpur Granny but these were just nice old ladies who were very sweet and seemed pleased when I called them Granny. My Goa Granny died before I was born, so this is about my Byculla Granny.

This means I had only one Granny.

My Byculla Granny looked like a Granny. She was fat and she was smiley and she smelled like a Granny.

Which means she smelled like something that was on the pot in the kitchen. She smelled so much of food that even the crows thought she was edible. One day I went into the kitchen and my Granny was sitting on a stool by the window, cleaning rice.

A crow came skirling in and sat down and pecked her hair. 'What a nuisance,' said my Aunty Irene. 'These crows are too much.'

'He's thissing,' said my Granny.

My Byculla Granny grew up in Goa. The family was very poor, so she was sent to an orphanage. They didn't treat her very well there or send her to school, so she was schooled only upto the third standard. At the age of sixteen, she was sent to Burma to marry my grandfather. He also died before I was born. I don't think I was very lucky for my grandparents. There she learned a little Burmese and she could say a few lines when she was angry.

Then the Second World War broke out and every country seemed to want to take over another country's land. To be fair, everyone had been doing this for a hundred years or more. Britain had taken over India, for instance, and Sri Lanka and Pakistan and Burma and Bangladesh. Germany marched into Abyssinia and Poland and Belgium. Japan thought, Yum, yum, here I come, and marched into Singapore and the Philippines and Burma.

So my grandfather walked from Burma to India and my Granny came by boat. The boat landed in Calcutta and my grandmother learnt some Bengali. When her husband got to Calcutta, they all came to Bombay and everyone was speaking English, including her children, who were studying in English-medium schools. And the maid spoke Marathi. And the neighbours spoke Hindi. And her mother still spoke Konkani. They said their prayers in Latin.

All these languages bumped about in her head and so she just didn't bother, and said, "thissing" or "thatting" whenever a word skipped out of reach.

But you knew what she was going to say. Everyone did. I don't know how. It was magic. Family magic. Every family has some.

'Where's my shirt?' my uncle Joseph would ask.

'I put it on your thissing,' Granny would say.

(On your bed.)

'It's not there.'

'Then you must have taken it for thissing and left it there. (Taken it when you went for a bath.) Not there? What not-there-not-there? You got eyes or thissing?' (Eyes or potatoes?)

Then my Granny would go into Uncle Joseph's bedroom and lift up the towel he had thrown down after a bath and there his shirt would be and he would smile and put it on and go to school.

So when she said that the crow is only thissing, Aunty Irene knew she meant "hungry".

'Oh, they'll eat anything,' she said. 'I once saw a snake eating someone's snot.'

'Only you see things like that,' said my Granny.

'What are you saying, Maan Berthe?' said Aunty Irene, opening her eyes wide. She was not really my aunty but her father had married my grandmother's sister-in-law's third cousin, who had died. He married again, this time someone quite unrelated to any of us, and had three children. Aunty Irene was the third child and she was nanny to some German children for years until they had to go back to Germany. She had no job in Bombay, so she came and stayed for a few days before going back to Goa. She had intended to stay one more week but it ended up being seventeen years. But that was the kind of house my Granny kept.

Now, without too many words, my grandmother's stories were very short. Here they are.

On Saving

Jenny had a penny.
She spent her penny.
She didn't have any.
Jenny had a penny.
She kept her penny.
Then she got another penny.
And another penny.
Now she had many.

Attulem and Bittulem

Attulem and Bittulem went to the jungle.
They met a tiger.

Attulem gave one fart and the tiger's left eye fell in.

Bittulem gave one fart and the tiger's right eye fell in.

And they went home and lived happily ever after.

I always thought this story missed a little something, so I decided to add some bits to it.

Attulem and Bittulem (revised)

Attulem and Bittulem went to the jungle.

They met a tiger.

Attulem gave one fart and the tiger's left eye fell in.

Bittulem gave one fart and the tiger's right eye fell in.

But as they went home, they heard the tiger weeping.

So they ran back and said,

'Tiger, tiger burning bright,

In the forest of the night,
What loud wails and creepy cries
What has happened to your eyes?'

The tiger said,
'Attulem, you stupid girl.
Bittulem, you silly churl.
There are a thousand girls like you.
Of tigers there are very few.
Now that you've knocked out my eyes,
I will fetch a decent price,
A poacher's going to take me home
And cut me into bits and bones.'

Attulem and Bittulem said,
'Oh we are so very sorry.
Wait till we bring daddy's lorry
We'll take you to a vet we know
And have your eyes back on the go.'

The tiger said,
That would be really kind

I will bear that in mind
And when I see a human child
I will be all meek and mild.
I won't even take a nibble
Even if I begin to dribble.

And so Attulem and Bittulem took the tiger home and got his eyes fixed up, and returned him to the wild, and everyone was happy.

I wish I had written down all the things my Granny told me. I didn't. You can. Go on then. Buy a notebook and start writing: Things my grandparents told me.

LOUDER THAN WORDS

Maegan Dobson Sippy

What does a curly-haired, chain-smoking, tea-drinking, impossible-to-keep-quiet-seventy-something-Scotswoman have in common with a

Bhojpuri-speaking, mild-mannered Indian sixty-five-year-old, who grew up in a UP village so small, you can't even find it on a map? Not much, you might think. Except that they were both my grandmothers. Granny Pat, my British father's mother, and Nani, my Indian mother's mother.

The rhythm of my early years was marked by their comings and goings. Granny would pitch up on a flight from Edinburgh just after Diwali, keen to escape the Scottish winter. By spring she'd have returned, to be followed in quick succession by Nani, whom we'd usually collect on our Holi visit north, bringing her back to Bangalore's more temperate climes before Lucknow's searing summer began.

Obviously, they'd met each other. My parents' wedding album confirmed this, with photos showing them proudly standing on either side of Ma and Pa, accompanied by their respective husbands—grandfathers who had both died before I had a chance to remember them. Nani in a gilt-edged, maroon-coloured sari, and more gold than I've ever seen her wear, and Granny in what can only be described as a resplendent turquoise evening gown, and matching earrings almost touching her shoulders.

Yet, despite the pictures, it seemed obvious to all of us that overlapping visits were to be avoided at all costs. 'I don't think my mother even knows that women smoke,' Ma hissed to Pa as they carefully replaced all the bottles of red wine in their drinks cabinet with bottles of soda water before Nani's imminent arrival. 'And besides, what will they do, share a bed?'

This was the year of my youngest brother's birth, which made me twelve, and infinitely qualified to both eavesdrop, and to chip in with my own opinions. 'What about the snoring?' I added, 'Nani won't be able to sleep!' Mine was the voice of experience, having spent a week of the last summer with Granny Pat on a camping trip. There's not much you can hide in a trailer tent.

'Whatever are you doing?' Granny asked, sailing in from the terrace in a kaftan, cup of tea in one hand, book in the other. She sighed. It was a fact universally acknowledged in the family that Pa and his mother were on opposite ends of the spectrum when it came to what Granny called "giving a damn". 'A drop of brandy with hot water's just the ticket for indigestion,' she smiled. 'You worry too much. We'll get along just fine. We both just want to be around for the baby.'

Naturally this was followed by much spluttering from both parents. 'But how will you communicate?' This was Pa, in all fairness pointing out the pretty insurmountable language barrier. 'And what about *food?!'* Now it was Ma, worrying about whether the red chilli powder would need to be put back into circulation during her mother's visit, and what it might do to her mother-in-law's digestive track. All of five, Rehaan had little to contribute. And me? I was secretly hoping for drama—at least enough to distract my parents from their relentless focus on baby-ji, who at that point in time was, it has to be said, a little dull. I'd calculated that Holi and

Easter fell on the same weekend that year, so my hopes were high.

Predictably, things got off to a rocky start. The arrival back from the airport was definitely awkward, with neither Nani nor Granny knowing whether to hug or shake hands, and the compromise being a slightly odd combination of the two. Then, much stilted conversation, as the parents tried to make small talk, encouraging me and Rehaan to act as translators, and making unimaginative suggestions for suitable topics of conversation, along the lines of—'Ask your Nani to tell Granny Pat about her flight.'

We were relieved of these responsibilities within a few days, though, when we proceeded to take our duties too literally—much to Ma's disgust. I was more than happy to translate 'Why does she burp so loudly after eating?' from English into Hindi. But a giggling Rehaan outdid himself by perfectly translating '*Dal thoda kum do, waise bhi raat ko Granny-ji ka bahut paad nikalta hai*' into English as, 'Give Granny Pat less dal, it only makes her fart in her sleep.'

Somehow, though, I slowly came to realise that the dynamic between my two grandmothers was more natural when the parents were at work, and not hovering around worrying about their respective mothers. The nook in my bedroom which contained my desk bordered the terrace, and I was able to listen to the afternoon conversations they had over tea (in Granny's case) and chai (in the case of Nani).

'Oooo, monkeys! How exciting!' Granny would trill, pointing to the trees in the adjoining plot.

'Arrey! These creatures! They'll take the washing,' Nani would reply, neither aware that their respective stances on the animals in question were completely opposite.

Or Granny would wax lyrical about the joy of sunshine, while Nani, recognising the word "sun", would chip in with her own thoughts on the hardship of summer, before they'd both laugh and return to a companionable silence.

This must have been about the same time that they started venturing out together for "ladies' lunches". Being at school, I never accompanied them, but I liked to imagine their conversations. What did other diners think when the unlikely duo rocked up, and proceeded to shout good-naturedly at each other in a language the other didn't understand, all the while stealing food from the other's plate, and patting each other's hands every time they wanted to express affection?

Then there was the day I came home from school to find Nani attempting to teach Granny to knit, their heads bent over the wool together, and Nani clearly taking much delight in Granny Pat's dropped stitches and valiant attempts at straight lines. 'They're going to be baby booties!' Granny exclaimed, proudly holding up a curled length of fabric, while Nani half-giggled, half-grimaced behind her.

Or the day Nani discovered that rice pudding was basically kheer in disguise, and only required the addition of cardamom, a handful of raisins and extra sugar in order to make it palatable. Closely followed by Granny's parallel discovery

that if you added caramelised apples to *panjiri*[10], it was pretty much apple crumble—her absolute favourite. Many communal kitchen experiments followed, much to my stomach's satisfaction.

Despite the obvious affection between the Grandmas, we were all still slightly apprehensive about the impending Holi-Easter weekend, especially when both Nani and Granny, unbeknownst to the other, started to make elaborate food plans. On Granny's part, she discovered the existence of the Bangalore Ham Shop from a neighbour she met in the lift. After ticking off her son thoroughly for not alerting her to the possibility of bacon earlier ('How could you not tell me? I've been freezing and bringing it in my suitcase for years, but it never lasts!'), she began to plan what was essentially a Sunday Roast—the crowning glory of which would be roast pork (scratchings and all), accompanied by Yorkshire puddings and roasted vegetables.

Nani, on the other hand, had envisaged a vegetarian thali—with three different sabzi

[10] made from whole-wheat flour fried in sugar and ghee

varieties, two types of dal, and freshly cooked *puris*[11]. Plus, for dessert, the traditional *gujias*[12], which, being labour-intensive, we were all supposed to help make. Much hand-wringing from the parents later, it was decided that it was essentially up to me to explain the situation to the Grandmas—and to come up with a compromise.

Compromise always sounds like a dangerous sort of word. Don't you think? For me it makes me think about everyone making sacrifices, and no one being happy. Our Holi-Easter was the opposite. It started with an Easter egg trail for everyone in our society—in which searching for baskets of small, sugar-covered chocolate eggs was made all the more fun by having to avoid other children trying to smear coloured powder on your face. The winner (sadly not me, but the shy girl from the flat upstairs) was the one with the most eggs, and the cleanest face. She was awarded a massive pure chocolate egg, bought by Granny from the fancy hotel down the road.

The hunt was followed by gujiya preparation

[11] unleavened deep-fried Indian bread

[12] sweet dumpling made with semolina or wheat flour and stuffed with khoya

—slowly boiling the milk until it was solid, adding industrial quantities of sugar, all helping to pound the cashew nuts, and then combining everything with dried fruits. For the pastry, Granny's modification ('On account of my cholesterol—and better for you too, dears!') was to teach Nani how to make shortcrust pastry, so that we could then bake the filled parcels in the oven, rather than deep-frying them.

Our appetites duly worked up, Nani's fit-for-royalty thali was just what we needed for lunch … and distributing our gujiyas-with-a-twist to our favourite people in the apartment complex was about enough exercise to work up an appetite for the roast dinner—in which Nani both turned a blind eye to the five kilos of pig on the table, and discovered a hidden talent for making the fluffiest Yorkshire puddings going. Now that's the kind of compromise anyone can get on board with.

I think that's why autumn and spring remain my favourite seasons. Because even though Nani continued to come in the summer, and Granny would always "winter" (that was her turn of phrase) in Bangalore, after that year there were always a few magical weeks in March and October when these two wonderful women would overlap.

But that first year always stands out in my mind. That was the spring I learned a lot of things. That actions speak louder than words. That as different as you may be on paper, deep down you might just have something in common. That getting along is easy with good humour and a lack of preconceptions. Oh, and that if in doubt, make kheer. Or apple crumble. Or preferably both. But whatever you make, make it with love.

I wrote this when I was pregnant with my first baby, imagining what it might be like for a child to grow up with grandmothers from opposite sides of the world.

MEMORY TABLES

Saee Koranne Khandekar

As grandmothers go, she fit the bill perfectly. Her softly starched, block printed or sheer woven Chanderi sarees would whisper as she walked slowly around the house, depending heavily on her walking stick, her arthritic feet protesting every step. The four thin bangles around her wrist had thinned even more with age and hung loosely around her wrinkled wrist covered in paper-thin skin, and seldom made their presence heard. A lingering freshness of Yardley Lavender calmed you down as she hugged you after a hot, hurried walk from school to her softly illuminated house. Her wavy hair was always neatly pulled back in a bun that got scantier over the years but always looked just as graceful, a bobby pin or two holding it in place. A smile that reached the eyes—her loving yet mischievous eyes, a sense of beckoning that only grandmothers are capable of. Except, she wasn't my grandmother.

Phyllis Marr came into our lives as Radha Gore—my maternal grandmother's grandaunt; and therefore, my great-grandaunt. Together with Madhav Kaka, they formed our third set of grandparents; and were perhaps the most accessible of the lot because they lived in the same suburb and we got to see them more often. N-16 was just a ten-minute walk from school and thus closer than home. When one was particularly ravenous after school or had run out of rickshaw money or was too lazy to walk home, one hop-skip-jumped to Radha Kaku's house. Invariably, a parent would come and pick us up later or we would get a royal ride home in Madhav Kaka's roomy old Ambassador with pretty lace curtains that fluttered gently, gracefully, in a barely-there breeze as he drove slowly along Vashi's generous tree-lined roads.

There were always two things on the table at N-16—a spray of fresh flowers and leaves from her little garden, and food. The kitchen was hardly ever silent—food was always being made. Or being planned. Or being eaten! All my memories of her are associated with food. Something for an after-school snack. Something for the way home. Something, now that you're here.

I distinctly remember a time when amma had to go away to be with my aunt, who was very sick, and my brother and I stayed back so we weren't in the way and would be fruitfully occupied at school.

Baba would have to go to work all day and Ajji, our paternal grandmother, came to help for a few days. School hours ended at 6 p.m. and after a brief half-hour break, I would have to go to Bharatanatyam class in the same premises. Usually amma would come by with a change of clothes and a snack, and I would slip into dance gear in one of the deserted classrooms. While she was away, Radha Kaku offered to do snack duty. I carried my change in the school bag. At 6 p.m., I would walk out of the school gates and step into Madhav Kaka's Ambassador. I would be handed a cool, damp face towel to freshen up. Kaku always carried these on train journeys and long drives, neatly packed in a plastic bag. Those were the days before disposable wet wipes came into the market. Once suitably freshened up, the lace curtains on the windows were drawn up and I would change into my Co-optex material salwar kameezes, stitched by the local *darzi*[13], in the car. (I could have just as easily dashed back to school to do this, but one didn't ask questions back then.) By the time I settled back

[13] tailor

into my seat, a napkin (with an embroidered flower in the corner, nonetheless) would quietly make its way to my lap. A picnic basket full of variously sized *dabba*s[14] would be opened and a dégustation would begin. First, the mandatory milk—a glass bottle with a sunset-coloured plastic screw top lid, Bournvita embossed proudly across its diameter, filled with the malt powder-flavoured milk. The bottle would have been kept warm by wrapping it snug in a napkin. I would have attempted feeble protests had amma brought it along, but with Kaku lovingly *beta-beta*-ing me along, I couldn't.

Next, the main course—warm *aloo tikki*s[15] with a *dabbi*[16] holding ketchup or vegetable sandwiches with a fresh green chutney and crisp vegetables. Or cheese toasties. Or a paneer filling inside a warm, soft *phulka*[17], freshly made. These I would wolf down in part hunger and part greed. Kaku's cooking was always mildly spiced and full of flavour and warmth. Quiet sophistication whispered out of the

---

[14] boxes

[15] snack made out of boiled potatoes, onions and various curry spices

[16] tiny box

[17] flatbread made of wholemeal flour

simplest of dishes she made. Planning and cooking meals came naturally to her or so she made it seem because she never looked flustered or panicky when unexpected guests arrived. Standing at the stove, she never looked anxious about how the dish was turning out to be. She was always confident and happy that she was cooking for somebody. Even when her arthritis had severely reduced her movement, she would meticulously monitor the cooking or muster up the energy to sit at the dining table and line a pie dish or stretch pizza dough or dress a salad. She taught me the importance of birthday cakes. She always made the effort to bake a cake for everyone's birthday—even the house help's. I usually got a pie because amma would have baked me a cake and Radha Kaku would probably not have wanted to repeat a dessert. I remember, this once she hand-rolled each individual letter of "Happy Birthday" and stuck it on the crust of the apple pie before baking. With her severe joint pains, this must have been painful or at least annoying, but she knew it would make a child feel special, so she did it. It is something that has stayed with me all these years. I still make sure, no matter what, that every single person in the family gets a homemade cake for their birthday. And the joy on their faces is something I owe Radha Kaku.

Diametrically opposite was Ajji. Some people say she used to be a great cook, but unfortunately, by the time I was old enough to form any food associations with her, she was too sick to cook. She had already had her first stroke and paralysed two fingers on her right hand before I was born, and had slowed down tremendously. She cooked the most basic of meals for us when we visited. *Varan-bhaat*[18], a vegetable dish and *poli*s[19]. Sometimes chicken curry if my grandfather felt like cooking it. That's if we were visiting by ourselves. If our parents came along, amma cooked all the meals. One distinct condiment that I remember from her limited repertoire, however, is her carrot pickle. She made bowlfuls every now and then for days when she didn't have the energy to cook a side

[18] vegan Indian food preparation involving pigeon pea, split beans and rice
[19] flatbread

to go with rice or polis. Unlike most commercial carrot pickles, this one was thinly grated and not diced or cut into julienne. This made it more appealing to us as children and it wasn't quite as hot as the ones bought.

But there were advantages of not having Ajji taking charge of her kitchen. It meant that we had free reign. During summer vacations, the otherwise prohibited Rasna would be dutifully bought after much argument about the flavour between my brother and myself—I always wanted *kala khatta*[20] and he always wanted orange or mango (ugh!). One afternoon would be constructively spent in following the instructions carefully and making the concentrate. Then, one hunted for two clean bottles (glass, in those days—reused bottles of some squash or ketchup) with no smell, and a clean funnel. A tableful of Rasna spillage later, the bottles made it to the refrigerator and the bar would be set. We were allowed unlimited glasses of Rasna in the day and we experimented by squeezing extra lime

[20] ice-based dessert made by shaving a block of ice and adding black salt, lemon juice and the tangy sweet blackberry syrup

juice or sprinkling *chaat masala*[21] or whathaveyou. Most times, we were lucky.

Ajoba would sometimes bring out an old ice cream churner and we would make (rather, attempt) orange ice cream. It was always orange, I wonder why. We would innocently mix clotted cream (collected from the top of the morning milk) with sugar, orange segments and milk, and pour the mixture into the ice cream churner. It was an ancient contraption—an aluminum bowl with a plastic rotating blade inside. The movement of the blade was powered by electricity but the bowl needed to be kept in the freezer when in action. The long wire had to extend out of the freezer and to the plug point across the refrigerator. It was hilarious because the door of the old refrigerator was loose and would never shut properly. I think I can say with some confidence that we never saw a set ice cream. Eventually, we would run out of patience, pour the barely frozen ice cream into glasses and gulp it down like a shake.

---

[21] spice powder mix

Then, of course, there were the endless packets of jelly and custard. I would make various permutations and combinations of these two ingredients, sometimes adding Ajji's homemade sundried grapes, and at other times whatever fruit was handy. I would stealthily remove the prohibited glassware from the cupboards while Ajji napped; I set my concoctions in them just because I was fascinated by their shapes and designs, and there was something of a high to be got from using fancy old crockery that one wasn't supposed to know existed.

During Diwali, however, she made the effort to stand and make *chirote*[22] and *anarse*[23]—very tricky pastries that my Mum and maternal Granny never made. Not that Ajji's were perfect, but they were my only reference point and I grew to love them. For years after she passed away, I had absolutely no access to these two Diwali treats, and I missed them so much. Until a few years ago, when I looked up recipe books and attempted making

[22] a delicacy made of wheat flour rolled into layered circular shapes and then deep frying in ghee or refined oil; served as a dessert mainly in Karnataka and Maharashtra

[23] Indian pastry-like snack commonly associated with Diwali in Maharashtra and Bihar with ingredients including jaggery, rice, poppy seed and ghee

some of my own. I must say I had the advantage of all my fingers being intact, so mine were more technically "correct", but there was something about the imperfections in hers that I will always miss. Every time I pat the anarse delicately on a bed of poppy seeds, I will think about her petite figure, frail with diabetes and ill health, standing in her dark kitchen against the counter, determined to make something for the people she loved.

I can't talk about grandmothers without talking about my maternal great-grandmother, Mothi Aai. Nobody in the family can talk about food without talking about my great-grandmother, a *sugran.* Loosely translated from Marathi, it means "a woman who cooks well", but oh, she was so much more than that! A very petite figure clad in the softest, freshest-looking cotton nine-yard saree, a round and angelic face framed by fine hair formed neatly into a braised bun. She ran a large household with a handful of friends and relatives constantly camped for further studies or work in town. Her menus are legendary and even more legendary is her Escoffier-like passion about breaking down traditional *andaaz*[24] cooking and documenting it for posterity. She filled her journals with recipes and tips and wrote long, detailed letters to everyone from her daughters to her great-granddaughters (me!) talking about culinary and family traditions and things that influenced her cooking. At a time when cooks of all levels—commercial and otherwise—fiercely guarded their secret recipes to feed their ego, here was a woman who willingly shared what she knew.

As a young bride of eighteen, she learned cooking from the short period she spent with her mother-in-law, and then on her own, asking questions to neighbours and friends and friends' mothers-in-law and the chief cook who made *motichoor ladoo*s[25] for a wedding in the family. There were notes about how many people one cup of rice would be sufficient for—three; but not if you're making six other side dishes, in which case one cup would stretch to four adults and one child easily. There were notes about what was made as

---

[24] style

[25] an Indian sweet made mainly with tiny, sweetened, fried chickpea flour

rukhwat (decorative foods that are put up on display at weddings and thread ceremonies to show the craftsmanship of the women of the house) at so-and-so's wedding—enormous baskets crafted out of *chaklis*[26] and filled with multi-coloured *saandge* (sun-dried lentil fritters) for flowers. Leafing through her notes and letters is like getting lost in time. A simpler time, yet one that displayed such variety and expertise using limited means. No fancy equipment or ingredients. Community cooking came to the fore—nobody made Diwali *faraal*[27] in isolation. A distinctive feature of Mothi Aai's memoirs are the *ovis*—couplets that women composed and sang as they went about their everyday chores such as sorting grain or pounding spices. In her notebook are ovis that Mothi Aai composed in praise of her offspring. I don't remember her singing but I can imagine her composing them in her head as she single-handedly, quietly, rolled out a hundred *puranpolis*[28]

[26] a spiral shaped, pretzel-like savoury snack from India with a spiked surface

[27] a variety of savoury snacks traditionally made at home and eaten during Diwali and also served to guests

[28] an Indian sweet flatbread from Maharashtra

just because she was throwing someone a pre-wedding feast and her husband thought puranpolis would make the ideal treat.

A forward-thinking family meant she had to innovate. Her father-in-law, a medical practitioner dressed impeccably in a suit with a pocket watch to boot, loved an elaborate tea. Light. Served in a teapot, not strained directly into a cup. Just a spot of milk. One day, he decided he had had enough of elaborate meals, and that he would eat a light supper every evening. Mothi Aai tweaked traditional recipes to make whole-wheat pancakes (no Betty Crocker in the early 1900s!) and jacket potatoes a la Marathi—stuffed with green chutney!

A lot of Mothi Aai's instinctive understanding of flavours has seeped into Aai, my maternal grandmother. It is to this amazing woman that I owe everything I understand about food. I remember very clearly how she would be standing at her kitchen counter in her airy and bright South Mumbai apartment, patiently roasting semolina. I would be sent to the living room, quite a few feet away from the kitchen, my olfactics on call. My job was to sit in the living room and identify from the smell whether the semolina was being roasted for *uppit*[29] or *sheera*[30]—each demanding a different degree of toastiness!

In the summer vacations, I would sit on a tall stool and watch as she kneaded her poli dough to silken perfection, most often with water that had been filled in the morning's milk pot to make sure no milk is wasted. The lactose sweetness of the milk made her polis more of a meditative affair than a mere carbohydrate requirement. She would roll out hot, triangular, many-layered polis slowly and lovingly and pass them through the service window between kitchen and dining table, where my grandfather, brother and I would be eating our brunch before grandfather left for his office. We'd eat so many at once that she would have to tell us to take a break, eat a little rice and then reassess our poli requirement!

---

[29] Indian breakfast dish, cooked as a thick porridge, from dry roasted semolina or coarse rice flour

[30] semolina-based Indian sweet that originated in Karnataka

As I sat with her in the kitchen, she would regale me with stories of how her childhood nanny would sneak her and her cousins off to the hut at the back of the house and treat them to a simple meal of fire-roasted *bhakri*[31] rubbed with flecks of sea salt; sometimes, a fiery masala of raw garlic, chillies and coriander to add flavour and scandal! Or of how she had only heard of distant family whose secret recipe was to make paneer-like squares of unsweetened colostrum and add them to a delicately spiced gravy. It is these stories, I think, that taught me to first cook recipes in my head and then in the kitchen. To anticipate flavour pairings and think about how textures would react in different cooking methods. It taught me much more than any catering school could.

Aai's yellow (and yellowed) notebook was a journal she started keeping when she got married and went away to a far-off town with no access to mother or mother-in-law to educate her in cooking. A modern woman backed with modern education,

[31] round flat hard unleavened bread often used in the cuisine of Maharashtra

she wrote her recipes more scientifically, making sections in her book for the various courses. *Aloo bhaat*[32]—a recipe she got from Indore, two or three versions of *sambhar*[33], even more versions of *goda masala*[34], *godhi huggi*[35], two ways. But most important are her after-event notes. 'On so-and-so occasion, I made two cups of rice, two vegetables and … a lot is left over; perhaps I should make one vegetable lesser next time.' It is a habit she has tried to instill in me and I have noble intentions of employing it every time I entertain guests, but I have failed so far. One day, I will get down to doing it. Until then, I will look at her wrinkled hands and pester her to make just one more poli for me and slather it with her homemade ghee.

Apart from the short course in Bakery and Confectionery that I took in college, everything else I know about food is thanks to the many sets of grandparents I was lucky

[32] potato rice

[33] lentil-based vegetable stew cooked with a tamarind broth

[34] special spice blend unique to Maharashtrian cuisine

[35] wheat payasam or kheer

enough to have. Judging whether the rava[36] *has been roasted for sheera or upma just by smelling it in the living room, or identifying the gentle aroma of* garam masala[37] *when it is merely sprinkled over dal in its final cooking moments, or feeling special about eating a three-course meal with a serviette on my lap in a groaning old Ambassador parked outside the school gate, these priceless experiences are the real education I received. In my piece, I got to relive those special moments and be just a pampered little grandchild again.*

[36] wheat product and a form of semolina

[37] a blend of ground spices common in India

THE LADY AT CHUMMOTER

Sejal Mehta

The house sat at the corner of the lane. It was a big house. Two-storeyed. Old. Lived-in. A little courtyard sat in front of it. A garden with an archway, covered with green creepers and pink bougainvillea flowers. The gate was two doors with a latch. One that you swung shut from the top. These doors had a number in a circle. **74**. Chummoter.

All the memories I have of my grandmother—ma, as the kids knew her, *bachen*[38] to the rest—have their roots in this number.

She was the lady of **74**.

Ma lived at Chummoter for most of her life. And this house began to stand for everything she was: warm and forgiving, selfless to a fault, ever open, never judging. Under her reign, **74** became a living, breathing being, like Ma herself.

Very quickly after Ma made her home here, to the battalion of family members from across the world—and there were enough to form an army (this was a Gujarati family after all)—Chummoter became a place to roost, to study, to idle away vacations, to lodge at through college, to recuperate from disease or love (depending on the affliction at the time), to find a comforting lap to weep/

[38] a term of endearment

sleep on, to feed, to scavenge, (for the kitchen at Chummoter was never closed), to drop messages for each other, to sit on the swing and ponder, to meet potential suitors under a watchful chaperone.

Essentially, if there was a question rising in the family's collective conscience, it was largely believed that the answer would reveal itself in Chummoter's loving embrace.

Her years at 74 were her most formidable. Fiercely independent, she was outwardly accommodating, but inwardly tenacious. Ma owned the family not because she excelled at cooking and cleaning, and what in those days was considered ideal qualities in the daughter-in-law of the house, but because of her heart, which was as big as Chummoter, if not larger. She loved fiercely, without context, and threw open her home to everyone who needed it, despite being widowed at a tragically young age.

Born at the dawn of the First World War, Ma lost her parents when she was very young. Raised by her older sister, and a child of a difficult period in history, Ma entered her wedded home at the early age of eighteen. Even so, her understanding of the world and its inhabitants was remarkable. Immensely spirited at heart, and an accomplished athlete at fourteen, her thin, lanky frame, striking beauty and cascading ankle-length hair were the envy of the girls' sorority in school.

Ma dreamed of being a sportsperson when she grew up, but her time on the playground, along with her education, was cut short when she was married off. The norm of the time did not allow for a young girl like her, motherless even, to have an ambition of this (or any) stature.

As a child, or even later when she was a mother, she never complained about the swift and almost casual dismissal of her dreams except for that one time.

She attended a meeting for and by a women's organisation, and I know she was delighted to be there, excited and hopeful, for the first time in her life, to be part of a cohesive group of peers, sharing and participating in matters that concerned women.

74

There, she walked up to an acquaintance and attempted to strike up a conversation, but the woman looked at her and walked away without saying a word. She came home in tears, and said of the slight, just that one time, 'If I were educated, this would not have happened.'

She never spoke of it again, but these things shaped her attitude towards her children and grandchildren. She delighted in my independence and career choices, and encouraged my dreams, no matter what they were. Progressive beyond her time, she never faulted our clothes, our nights out, our almost fierce dedication to work. She was very proud of us all—she said work came first, then everything. She sent both her sons to study abroad and when both married American citizens, she accepted their decisions despite societal perceptions, and, in truth, her own wishes. All she said was, 'If that is what makes them happy, I am happy'.

When **74** was sold, Ma lost a part of herself. The large place being no longer manageable, it was decided that Chummoter would have to go.

The family collectively mourned the loss of their childhood, because there wasn't a single child in the family who had not at some point called Chummoter home and didn't feel an almost proprietorial claim over it.

The last few years of her life were the toughest for Ma, and I believe leaving **74** had a lot to do with it. She was aware, when she signed the sale, that home would never mean the same again. She lived in at a flat, and later with us in Bombay, and I know that those were the toughest years of her life, and her health had little to do with it. **74** had been hers, and she had belonged to it, too. Her independence, her comfort, her memories were all wrapped up in its tiled floors, in the garden, in the shortcuts to her family's homes around the place.

Here, in Bombay, she floundered. Her health deteriorated, and in answer to that, her will only got stronger. I believe something similar was happening with **74**, as it was razed to the ground, to make way for an apartment building that was ten floors high. At my home, I, with my impudence of youth, was not very good to her during her final years. I was short with her, impatient with her age, and at the end, resentful of her illness. I thought I knew better, as children often do. I saw only the old, stubborn woman, unable to come to terms with her restrictions. I forgot about the powerful matriarch, the years that she had triumphed over everything, the experience and wisdom she had and the sheer strength of her will.

These are all traits I had always wished for, but when faced with them hidden in the garb of an ailing grandmother who should (did) know better, I fought to tame them. As children, we study much, learn nothing, and just because we know how to speak a language better or go to school, we think that we know more than the ones who have lived through sheer experience; lives more difficult than we'll ever know. I have never forgiven myself for it.

Ma breathed her last in Bombay, surrounded by loved ones, our relatively large apartment almost unable to fit in the army of heartbroken Chummoter alumni who came to pay their respects.

It is a testament to the relationship we had with Chummoter that even today, when we talk about Ma, we see her in that house, in the kitchen, serving hot crumpled rotis dripping with ghee to grandchildren who sat in a line in the chowk, or helping the domestic help with their studies, paying for their children's careers, sitting on the swing on the front porch, and running her kingdom from her throne.

Today, when I pass **74**, it is no longer Chummoter, it is almost ugly in its transformation, sterile, non-committal, even aloof, but I'd like to believe that somewhere in the foundation, Ma's steely resolve and her unending ability to love lives on, and that the house still sighs when it thinks of the lady at **74**.

In the memory of a matriarch and her home, and all the childhoods—especially her oldest son Girin's—that contributed to this note.

BILLY

Sreedevi Gopakumar

'But it wasn't me who poured ink all over your shoes! It must have been Appu!'

Paru heaved a sigh of relief as Papa stormed

off to look for her younger brother. She had not meant to mess up Papa's shoes like that. It wasn't Paru's fault that she had mistaken an ink pad for boot polish, she reasoned. And then felt a twinge of fear—what if Papa figured out that it wasn't Appu, after all? What would she say then?

Paru stole a quick glance at the other person in the room, her grandmother. But Ammuma was in her chair by the window, lost in her cross stitch pattern. Just as Paru was about to make a run for it, Ammuma spoke up.

'Have you noticed something, Paru? Animals and people react in the same way to many things. We dance in joy, or cry out in pain and sorrow. But there is one emotion that animals handle with more dignity and grace than humans. And that is fear.'

'Animals can't possibly have more dignity that humans, Ammuma!' scoffed Paru.

'Well,' Ammuma replied as she continued with her embroidery. 'Humans and animals do the same things in the face of danger. They either freeze, flee or fight. But in humans, fear also has the power to warp hearts and twist minds. It convinces people to lie and put the blame on someone else. And that is something no animal would ever do—intentionally get another living soul in trouble just so they can escape.'

Paru squirmed uncomfortably. Had Ammuma caught her, after all?

'Do you know what happened to Billy the tomcat? No? Come sit next to me and I'll tell you.'

Paru settled down on the floor, and leaned comfortably against Ammuma's knee. Then as she ran her fingers through the little girl's hair, Ammuma began the tale of Billy the Belligerent who learnt a lesson.

'Billy the tomcat was known far and wide for his hunting skills. He lived a pampered life with his human family, but still hunted mice, pigeons and anything else that caught his fancy. Over the years his reputation grew and no animal or bird would go near Billy's apartment. Other cats and even dogs would tremble at the sight of Billy strutting about the compound. And Billy the Belligerent basked in the warmth of his power.

'But as the years went by, Billy found himself slowing down. His eyes weren't as sharp as they used to be. He couldn't pounce as high as he used to. His meals had reduced to milk and bread with the occasional fish thrown in. And once the animals in the neighbourhood realised that the old tomcat couldn't hunt anymore, they made their way into his apartment and stole food from right under Billy's nose!

'I can't let this go on,' thought Billy. 'I need to find a way to get them to come to me, because I certainly can't chase them anymore. What I need is an image makeover!'

'So Billy sat in the shade of the tulsi plant in the balcony, with his eyes firmly shut. Pigeons saw him and gurgled in mirth. Mice crept out to titter at him. But Billy stayed right where he was, lost in his own thoughts. And this went on for a few days.

'Finally, Mur-Mur, the little mouse, could take it no more. Was this the Billy she had heard so much

about—the marauder of mice, the persecutor of pigeons, the despair of dogs? Surely this Billy wasn't so bad. Inch by inch Mur-Mur crept out of her hiding place to see what Billy was doing.

'Billy's eyes were still tightly shut, but his nose twitched frantically as the little mouse came closer. Finally, he spoke in the calmest voice he could muster.

'Do not be afraid, little one! For I am no longer the mouse-murderer I used to be. My days are numbered, and as is the way of the world, I have surrendered myself to The Divine. No longer can I bear the thought of eating another one of God's creations! Henceforth I will spend my days meditating under this tulsi and sustain myself on the blandest of vegetarian food. Come closer, little one. You have nothing to fear at all.'

'So Mur-Mur slinked closer and closer, till she could see the old tomcat's whiskers quivering, and hear his ancient heart thudding. Suddenly, Billy let out a blood-curdling screech and pounced on little Mur-Mur!

'Ha!' he cried. 'I've got you now! So you thought I was too old and feeble to hunt anymore, eh? I'll teach you to mock me!' he hissed as he squeezed poor Mur-Mur harder.

'Eep! Eep!' squealed Mur-Mur in pain and terror. 'Please let me go, Billy! I'm too small to make a proper meal for someone as big as you. I'm not even big enough to be an appetizer! Oh, please, please let me go!'

'Billy considered the little creature thrashing about in his paws. 'Hmmm ...' he mused. 'Maybe you do have a point, after all. But I don't think other mice are nearly as adventurous or trusting as you. I'll tell you what—go back home and tell your family and friends that I am your new best friend. Bring them over to see me up, close and personal. And I will feast on the fattest and juiciest of them all. Promise me this and I will let you go—your life for theirs!'

'Yes, yes, Mr Billy, sir!' cried poor Mur-Mur. 'I give you my word—I'll convince everybody to come and meet you! Just let me go now, and I assure you, you will never go hungry again!'

'And so Mur-Mur escaped by the skin of her teeth. She raced back to her dark, warm home and cowered in a corner as she caught her breath. Once she had calmed down a little she began to plan out her course of action. Perhaps she could stand up at the next Monthly Mouse Meeting and talk about her new best friend Billy. Or maybe she could introduce him as her guru, Billy the Benevolent. She could offer to take others to see the old cat, to see for themselves that he had turned over a new leaf. Everybody would believe her, as Mur-Mur was known to be an honourable mouse.

'But even as she laid these plans, Mur-Mur realised that she would never go ahead with them. There was no way that she would lie and get another poor soul into deadly danger. The only reason somebody would believe her fibs would be because they believed her too good to lie. And she would not take advantage of that.

'So Mur-Mur slowly made her way back to Billy. The tom raised an eyebrow when he saw her slink into view. There were no other mice in sight.

“‘Let me guess,’ said Billy in a deceptively calm voice. ‘You could not find anybody as foolhardy as yourself.’

“‘You sneaky, snarky, snivelling stinker!’ cried Mur-Mur. ‘I will not let you turn me into a cheat! I’ll never trick anybody the way you have deceived me! You can eat me if you wish. But always remember, this little mouse is twice the man you’ll ever be!’

‘And Mur-Mur closed her eyes tightly as she waiting for Billy’s paws to grab her. But as the minutes slowly ticked by, Mur-Mur heard something that sounded distinctly odd. Was it … but it couldn’t be … Mur-Mur slowly opened her eyes. It *was* Billy crying! The old cat was leaning against the tulsi plant, his head bowed in shame.

‘You’re right, little one,’ whimpered Billy as tears trickled down his snout. ‘I may have been the most feared creature in the neighbourhood, but I could never be as brave as you. Nor as selfless. Please forgive me. Please, let us be friends.’

'But Mur-Mur raced back home, glad to have escaped with her life. She wasn't about to fall into the same trap twice!'

Ammuma stared out the window for a few minutes while Paru ruminated over the story. Then, as her grandmother picked up her embroidery again, Paru got to her feet and gave her a tight hug.

'What are you going to do now, Paru?' asked Ammuma.

'Something I should have done a while ago, Ammuma,' replied Paru as she set off to look for Papa.

Ammuma smiled in quiet pride.

Most people have never seen my grandmother do anything except fine embroidery and extraordinarily complicated cross stitch. Only those closest to her knew that under her placid exterior lay the toughest person we had seen in close quarters. Ammuma was never one to entertain fear or idle chit-chat. In fact, as a young mother in her thirties, she had famously crushed a cobra to death with a large rock and gone quietly back to her cooking while the many men of the family gaped in horror and fascination. She told me the story of Billy when I was about nine or so, but I had forgotten about it until my friend's grandmother told me her version a few days ago. In retrospect, this little story captures much of my Ammuma's spirit—buck up and be a hero. With as little drama as possible, please.

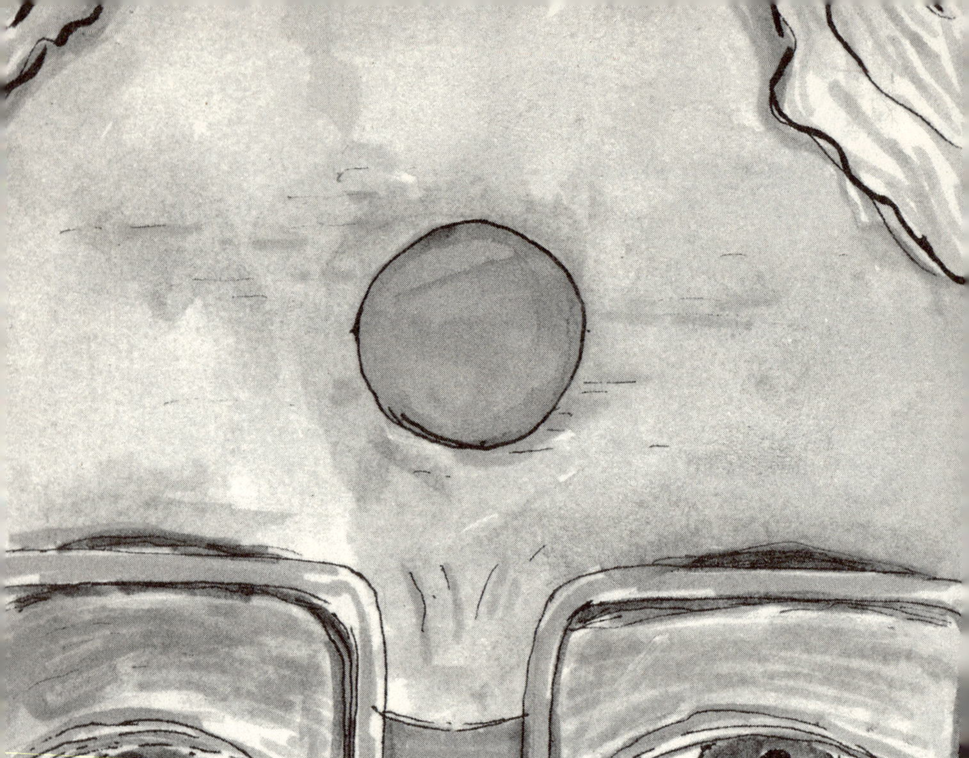

PAATI

Vidya Balachander

There is an old black-and-white photo of my childhood that flashes to my mind when I think about Paati. I am a round baby with formidable thigh folds, nestled in the crook of my grandmother's arm, posing next to a plump jackfruit in the garden. Paati is looking straight into the camera, her gaze direct and open, her face unadorned except for a brick-red *pottu*[39] in the centre of her forehead. Her cotton sari is drawn snugly yet modestly around her waist, and you can't help but notice how youthful she looks, her feet firmly planted and her shoulders square and upright. That's the image of Paati I hold in my mind's eye, because even in later years, when life had shrivelled her and the folds of her skin hung loosely to her tiny frame, she still held her own—both in person and in pictures.

Paati, my maternal grandmother, shone with a brilliance that belied her slight build. Born into abject poverty and forced to abandon schooling at a young age, she never stopped yearning for knowledge—knowing that it held the key to a world beyond her hearth.

As a toddler who often invaded the snug space between my grandparents at night, I remember

[39] a bindi or red dot worn on the centre of the forehead

falling asleep to the sight of Paati bent over a stack of *Kumudam* and *Mangayar Malar* magazines. It was an unfailing nightly ritual: after having brushed her teeth and changing into a dotted *sungudi*[40] sari, sandpapered by age into softness, she would settle into her corner of the bed, slowly thumbing through the Tamil magazines that she would receive by snail mail. It wouldn't be until years later, when words became my own currency of dealing with the world, that I would realise the worth that they held for her.

The stories of our grandmothers usually portray one truth: they made the most of what they had—or what they were given—with plucky resolve and matter-of-fact practicality. But even by that standard, the arc of Paati's life was an extraordinary one. Married while still in her late teens to Thatha, her first cousin (a common practice in those times), a gentle, generous and ambitious man who rose to the highest rungs of the Indian Administrative Service, Paati trailed in his illustrious shadow. When Thatha

[40] cotton fabric of Madurai

was appointed to the service of Maharaja Holkar of Indore, before India acquired independence, Paati left behind her hometown in Kerala and moved all the way to the Hindi heartland. Now, having taken a leap of faith to move to a new country myself, I have a better grasp of just how daunting it might have been for Paati. For a young lady whose contours of the world were tightly drawn around her little village with a waterfall, it must have been dizzying and disorienting to suddenly find herself in a sprawling palace—Thatha's official accommodation in those days—in a new city, surrounded by the cadences of an unfamiliar tongue.

A few years later, when my mother was a teenager, they would move again—this time to the rarified neighbourhood of Altamount Road in Mumbai. I don't know why I never thought to ask Paati about the city where I spent nearly two decades of my life and still count as my first love. Perhaps it was because I was so fascinated by the stories of what came next. Even in her most outlandish dreams, Paati could not have imagined

that she would one day live in West Africa, with the golden sands of the Sahara sprawling out in her backyard. Yet, for several years when my mother was in high school, Paati bounced around from one country to another in French-speaking West Africa, accruing the stories that we would one day listen to in wide-eyed fascination. In the grainy, black and white photos of those years that we viewed on a clunky View-Master, Paati stood out gracefully in her silk saris among her new-found African friends, her pottu resolutely in place. Given her fierce intellect, she quickly picked up French, always slipping in the casual *'Qu'est que ce?'* in conversation right until she passed away two years ago, at the ripe old age of ninety three.

Paati's universe expanded from a pin prick on the map to the immeasurable expanse of the Sahara, virtually overnight. I like to imagine that she collected the experiences with care, wrapping them in the fragile muslin of memory and stashing them away. They would serve well in later years, when, with the same suddenness that marked their departure, Thatha and Paati would close the charmed chapter of their lives that unfolded in Africa, and return to Ratlam. With the gift of perspective that I have today, I might have asked Paati how she felt about the sands shifting beneath her feet so decisively, whether she missed the musical lilt of French spoken on the streets of Togo or picnics by the river in Niger. Did she wish she could have lingered, perhaps stayed a little longer?

Like many women of her generation, Paati had little control over the trajectory of her own life. And yet, even though her destiny was inextricably tied to Thatha's, her personality and passions were resolutely her own. By the time I was old enough to be sentient of how different my beloved grandparents were from one another, they were already septuagenarians. A near-fatal accident and deteriorating eyesight meant that Paati now took fewer walks in the enormous garden laden with tamarind, jackfruit, mango and custard apple trees.

Yet, even when she could no longer freely embrace the fleeting beauty of the changing seasons, she never stopped seeking it out.

The plants in the verandah became her sanctuary, and she would spend several slow, deliberate moments every afternoon tending to them and watching them grow. In the summer, when the days in Ratlam were flattened by dry heat, she would occasionally accompany us to the terrace in the evenings, always pausing contemplatively before the fire engine-red gulmohar tree in full blossom. It would take years before I understood just why she was so drawn to those blossoms, fluttering in the breeze like a red cloud. By then, I had moved away from my parents' home to work in Mumbai. Floundering for a sense of rootedness in the city, I would often find myself longing for the simplicity and cosiness of my early life in Ratlam.

Memory is an unreliable ally, embellishing some details and blurring others at will. I am often alarmed when memories that once seemed so clear and accessible now seem a little foggy, like far-away reflections in a rear-view mirror. There is so much about Ratlam that I have forgotten now, years since both my grandparents passed away. Yet, I remember those late summer afternoons on the terrace, when the sun had lost its afternoon vigour, and a cool breeze rustled the ripe tamarind pods hanging from the tree in our porch. I remember Paati peering at the gulmohar blossoms with intense concentration through her thick glasses. I remember her soft hands that smelled of gokul sandal powder, and that her pottu was never a brash red, but always a mature maroon.

Curiously, I never associated Paati with cooking. My mother tells me she had her signature recipes —like a tangy *puli inji* or tamarind-ginger relish— that she prepared with exacting care, but I don't remember tasting it. Even at a very young age, I recognised that Paati was special because she saw beauty in the mundane everydayness of life. When I had just begun school, she would bathe me in her bathroom with powder blue patterned tiles, always pausing to point out the silhouettes that she saw on them. She would discern puffy white clouds, a boy holding a balloon and even a little girl like me walking to school. She would weave in those abstract reflections with stories of my mother's childhood, and I would be transported to a different time and place.

Paati didn't need to own things to take pleasure in them—when she died, her belongings included a few silk saris, a handkerchief, a small Ganpati idol and a few photographs. All her worldly possessions could fit neatly into a small cloth bundle. She had the ability to find complete satisfaction in the saturated *rani* pink or fuchsia tone of a sari someone was wearing, or the pitch perfect flavour of a dish that she enjoyed eating. She laughed freely, clapping her hands like a child when delighted. But when she was wounded, she could slice you to shreds with her sharp, acerbic tongue.

As the years pass, I realise that I am like Paati in so many ways. There are few things that can give me more pleasure than colour—the unabashed pink of bougainvillea, the lemony yellow of laburnums, the turquoise radiance of a kanjeevaram. I wield words with hurtful precision when I am feeling vulnerable, and I laugh a giggly, girly laugh that has come to be trademark in many ways. I wonder what Paati would make of these comparisons. Of all her grandchildren, I was both the youngest and the most spoilt—and she indulged and chastised me in equal measure. Yet, now that she is no more, I would like to take pride in what I consider her legacy. Paati was an unconventional woman with refined tastes and a down-to-earth endurance of the many curveballs that life threw at her. If I were someday described in those terms too, I would consider my life a well-lived one.

Although I spent my charmed early childhood with Paati, my maternal grandmother, it wasn't until I was an adult that I fully appreciated how unique she was. This essay is a dedication to the determined, resilient, brave and beautiful woman that she was—it's a way to remember her by.

FIGHT YOUR OWN BATTLES

Zainab Sulaiman

Grandma hates my friends.

Reena is large and clumsy and can usually be found hanging around our house at lunchtime. Arti whispers in my ear a little too much for her liking. Antony, our maid's son, is a useless smart alec who has no right to follow his mother to work, leave alone play with her boss's granddaughter.

'Just because Antony's poor, you don't like him!' I lob back into Grandma's court. 'And Reena can't help it if she likes to eat. God's made her like that!'

'Don't argue, Little Egg,' Grandma replies, though she doesn't meet my eye. 'Now come inside. Enough playing for the day.'

'Five more minutes!' and I bound out of the door, clear the first five steps and alight on the landing, as nimble as a kitten, as light as a feather. There are five more flights of stairs to go to reach the bottom and I soar through the air as I effortlessly clear each one; and I am flying, ever faster, ever higher, and it's the second-best feeling in the world.

For the best feeling in the world is to play. There can never be enough play for me, ever. I wonder how adults get through life without playing, and I promise myself that I will always play, always, no matter how big I grow or how old I get.

Arti is in the midst of throwing a tantrum when I arrive. Apparently Reena has drawn the hopscotch boxes too large and she can't hop across. 'Not fair!' she yells at Reena, hands on hips, an angry fire-breathing dragon with a shock of short curly hair.

'Let me try.'

I snatch the smooth grey stone out of Arti's hand and expertly lob it at the furthermost box—it lands inside and I hop across the boxes at top speed, grab the stone and return.

'It's fine—don't complain.'

The dragon turns on its chubby heels and stalks off in the direction of its lair.

Reena and I are soon in the thick of things and don't notice that our enemies have crept up alongside the low wall that separates my house from the neighbours: these are my neighbour's horrible sons and a few of their low-life friends. And so we get the shock of our lives when a sudden bursts of 'Boo!' 'Yay!' 'Hah!' and other such nonsense come hurtling at us, even as they run off back to wherever they came from, laughing and shouting at how *puski*[41] we are.

'Idiots! Don't think you're too funny! *You* are the cowards!' I shout at the four or maybe five retreating backs.

The boys live to sneak up on us and catch us unawares. However, they don't mess about too much, as I'm known for my lively temper and sharp tongue, and so it doesn't take much for them to take to their heels.

'Come on, Priya. *Now*!'

Grandma's losing patience and I hurriedly say bye to Reena, who's looking a little sad at this abrupt departure as, for a change, she is winning.

'Grandma!' I burst in, indignant and angry. 'Those boys are always troubling us. Why can't you do something?'

'Don't play downstairs then,' is the useless reply. 'Why can't you read a book or do a nice puzzle? Always running around like an urchin!'

[41] cowardly

Mumbling 'you're so mean' (which Grandma ignores), I head off for my bath. If only Grandma could unleash herself on those stupid twits—what fun that would be!

For Grandma is no ordinary little old lady who ruffles children's hair and passes candics. She is a large unsmiling Englishwoman who only ever wears steel-blue cotton sarees and has steel-grey hair to match, that is always tied in an impeccable knot on her head, as she gazes down from a height at her grandchildren who she loves more than anything else in the world.

Just not enough to defend them when they most need her, I grumble.

***

Atul was tall, wore glasses and was eleven years old. He had just moved into the neighbourhood and lived in the block of flats a few lanes away. He had walked into the compound one morning and stood over Antony and me as we laboured over an ant hospital that we'd decided to erect in case any of the many busybodies crawling around the compound might be in need of some timely aid. We were constructing the building from twigs and leaves but it was refusing to stand on the wobbly sticks we had erected, and though we had dug deep into the earth to make the foundation strong, the walls refused to stay up.

'Prop them up with stones,' Atul instructed us and knelt down to show us how to do it. Instantly the hospital took shape, and the three of us got busy hunting for our patients, and even though our intention was just to give them a little break from the rigours of their hard lives, most of them protested this move vigorously and, rather ungratefully, jumped off their twig stretches and stalked off home.

Antony, much to Grandma's obvious distaste, was spending the bulk of his Dussehra holidays with me—poor Mary Ma had simply no other place to leave him, and tried her best not to notice Grandma's scowls and growls every time Antony popped up—and so we'd take ourselves off to the compound to spend the mornings rooting around for hidden treasures.

Atul would join us in the morning as he had tennis-guitar-tuitions and God-knows-what-else after lunch, and as he also didn't like Reena and Arti very much, I had to explain to them that it would be better if we played in the evenings.

Arti had made a face and walked away saying she wasn't available to play when it suited my whims and fancies, but Reena had nodded and said nothing, though she looked hurt and wasn't her usual self when we played later in the evening.

I tried not to think too much about her small face, and as the mornings always sped away doing exciting stuff, like playing with Atul's chemistry lab kit that his father had gifted him—with real test tubes and even a small Bunsen burner—or playing video games in his room (he had his own TV), this was not hard to do.

Then one day everything changed.

Antony and I were digging away at a big lumpy opaque thing in the compound, when Atul joined us and helped yank it out. It was squishy, not too soft and not too hard, and a dull moonshine radiated from within. We were convinced it had fallen out of the skies and couldn't wait to head off to Atul's room to examine it with the full array of his scientific equipment.

'Come, Antony, let's go,' Atul looked at Antony, and turned and began to walk away.

'I'm coming too,' I shouted, scrambling to my feet, but he turned around and gave me a funny look.

'No. Only Antony,' he said, and turned away again.

I looked at Antony, who looked like he wanted the earth to open and swallow him up, but with a helpless shrug of his thin shoulders he followed Atul to his apartment, leaving me standing behind, tears filling my eyes even as I furiously willed them not to.

***

It was the boys: they'd got to him somehow.

He'd taken to playing cricket with them in the late evenings; this was around the time I was ordered to come in for dinner and I wasted no time making myself scarce, waving a quick goodbye to

Reena and Arti, relieved to have a valid excuse to disappear from the scene.

Antony had stopped coming, now that the holidays were over, and even though at first I had been very hurt by Atul's behaviour, I slowly got over it. It helped that I hardly saw him any more—and even when I did, he always behaved as if I didn't exist—and so I went back to playing hopscotch or jumping rope with the girls. And to my undying gratitude, Reena and Arti didn't bring up my shameful behaviour and acted as if nothing had happened at all.

Then one day as we were playing an exciting new game of corks—each player had to put down three used bottle corks in the centre of a circle and then everyone took turns at knocking them out of the circle with a smooth flat stone; the winner was the one who could knock the most out—he reappeared.

'Don't cheat!' I rounded on Arti as she tried to knock the Thumbs Up cork out of the circle with the tip of her rubber chappal; Reena and I had been playing rock-paper-scissors to decide who went first, and she'd taken her chance.

'I'm not cheating!' she retorted and threatened to take away her corks if we wrongly accused her anymore—she had the most corks; Reena and I had just two each—and as this forced us to argue the point *without* seeming like we were arguing the point, we didn't notice the boys creep up in the passageway over the wall.

They had left us alone over the last few weeks—they'd been away during the vacation—and so we were taken totally unawares.

'Cheaters!' they bellowed in one voice. 'Cheaters! Cheaters! Cheaters!'

Arti burst into tears, which led to joyful whoops of 'Weepers! Weepers! Weepers!'

'Stop it!' I yelled, rounding on the lot to shoo them away as usual, and found myself staring straight into Atul's eyes. He had a smirk on his face and though he turned to follow the other figures that were running pell-mell down the passageway, he walked slowly, as if to show me that *he* wasn't scared, that my shouting had no effect on him.

***

'Why aren't you going down to play?' Grandma looked at me over her spectacles, as I lay sprawled across the armchair, reading *Five Run Away Together* for the fifth time.

'Don't feel like.'

'But that girl, the big one, she's calling you.'

'I don't care. I'm not going.'

She studied me for a moment—I ignored her and pretended to read my book—and when I refused to look up, she went back to knitting the blue cap that would be shortly shoved over my head whenever I stepped out, as December was around the corner.

'Priiiyaaa … Priiyaaa …'

Arti's voice joined in and I sighed and got to my feet.

'Coming!'

It was no fun playing in the compound nowadays because it almost always ended the same way: the boys lined up on the wall, laughing and joking as if we didn't exist, though we were just a few feet away, passing comments that they claimed were not about us—a sneering 'Fatty-Bombalatty!' when Reena tripped on the skipping rope and was declared out, or a theatrical whispered chant 'Crybaby-Crybaby-Crybaby' that always brought tears to Arti's eyes though she turned her back to them and tried to get the corks out of the circle, or hoots of 'Hey! Ho! Hey! Ho!' when I was skimming across the hopscotch boxes, quickly looking away when I glared at them.

But they no longer ran away, just continued to sit on the wall, their ringleader wearing an insufferable look on his face.

Today, though, the wall was empty and we decided to take turns to swing on the rubber tube that my father had rigged up; the tube hung from a metal ring that was fixed to the underside of the balcony that jutted out over a portion of the compound.

'Oh no, they're coming,' Reena whispered a little later as Arti swung herself round and round, her face growing as red as a tomato.

I took a deep breath and turned my back on them. Today I wasn't going to let them bother me: let them scream and hoot all they wished.

'Ignore them,' I whispered back, and we kept our eyes on the tube and continued to exchange notes on how we could best convince our mothers to allow us to wear make-up—at least on our birthdays.

And after a long time, the three of us began to have fun again, as we giggled about the mascara Arti had "borrowed" from her mother's dressing table—we planned to put it back by the weekend—and tried to decide if we should attempt a trial run before that, when a small stone whizzed past my ear and another hit Reena in the back.

'Ouch!' Reena yelled and we spun around towards the wall. The boys were suddenly very interested in something the fellow in the middle held in his hand, but their muffled laughter was enough to give them away.

'Stop that!' I shouted, but my voice cracked. Reena was rubbing her back and tears filled her big eyes; Arti had begun to sniffle.

'Stop that or …' but I choked on the words. For this was a new fight that we could never win: the boys were too big, too many and too strong for the three of us.

And then suddenly, 'Ayyyy!' something like a thunderbolt shot through the air and everyone looked up in shock, but none more than me.

For Grandma had appeared on the balcony and was glowering like a meteor about to explode.

'Stop that! Now! Or I will call the police!'

It took the boys all of two seconds to scramble off the wall and hit the ground running; this time Atul following at a healthy pace.

'Play Little Egg,' Grandma lowered her voice a few notches, but it was still loud enough for the entire neighbourhood to hear. 'You girls play. No one will trouble you from now onwards.'

***

'Atul wants to say bye,' Antony looked at me sheepishly from the threshold. 'He's leaving for Amreeka.'

I stepped out and came face to face with Atul. I hadn't seen him since that fateful evening.

'Er … bye,' he said, looking at me expectantly.

'Bye …' I was at a loss for words.

The three of us stood around silently for a few long seconds and then he turned and went down the stairs.

'Those other boys made fun of him for playing with you,' Antony mumbled. It was Sunday and he was accompanying Mary Ma to church, after she finished her morning's work. 'Called him a sissy. Maybe that's why …'

I nodded. It didn't matter now but at one time I'd wanted nothing more than to be friends with the strange skinny boy who was walking away without a backward glance.

'Want to play corks?' I asked, glancing over my shoulder to see if Grandma had heard.

She'd expressly forbidden me to play with "that boy" as soon as she'd spied Antony hanging around in the compound below; he'd instantly disappeared behind a clump of mast trees.

'OK,' his eyes gleamed and he jingled his pockets stuffed to the brim with corks of all shapes and sizes; he'd come prepared.

'Grandma, I'm just coming!' and I ran down the stairs, soaring through the air as I cleared one flight at a time, Antony following right behind.

My grandmother was an extremely special person in my life and this story is a small tribute to her love and support for me throughout my childhood.

Sharu Ajji's SPICY PICKLE ♥ RECIPE

WITH LOVE pranita KOCHAREKAR

I dedicate this to my beloved late grandaunt. I spent most of my childhood eating her delicious self-discovered recipes. She was not only a great cook but also a humble, selfless and caring being. I'm sure she would love to have a part of her in every kitchen.

INGREDIENTS

1 cup oil
1/2 tsp turmeric
1/2 cup rock salt
5 tsp pickle masala
1 tsp mustard seeds
1/2 tsp asafoetida (hing)
10-12 fenugreek seeds (methi)
4-4$^{1/2}$ tsp split mustard seeds
1/2 kg raw mango (approx. 3 cups of chopped raw mangoes)

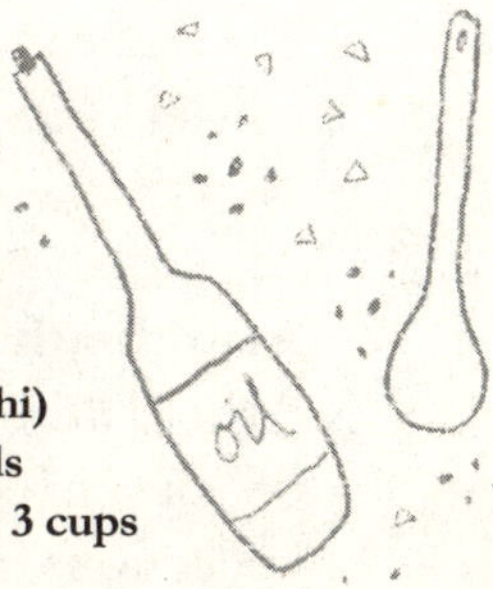

RECIPE

READY!

On day 1, mix the raw mangoes, turmeric, rock salt, spilt mustard seeds and pickle masala. Leave it overnight.
On day 2, heat 1 cup of oil. Add mustard seeds, asefoetida and fenugreek seeds. Allow the mixture to heat for a while.
Let it cool for 30 minutes.
Add the mixtures from both the days and mix well. Spicy, delicious pickle is ready to eat! (Refrigerate at all times.)

ABOUT THE AUTHORS

Andaleeb Wajid

Andaleeb Wajid has written several novels in the past seven years. Her Young Adult novel *When She Went Away* was shortlisted for The Hindu Young World GoodBooks Award 2017. Andaleeb is a full time writer and a creative writing facilitator at Nutcracker Workshops.

Anjali Nayar

Anjali Nayar is a journalist and author of children's books who currently lives in New York. She is also an award-winning filmmaker and illustrator. Her work has been published by *Scholastic*, *Puffin*, *The Big Roundtable*, *India Together*, *Hardnews* and *The Brooklyn Ink*. She recently completed her master's degree in Journalism from Columbia University, New York.

Arundhathi Subramaniam

Arundhathi Subramaniam is the award-winning author of eleven books of poetry and prose. Her most recent collections include a book of poems, *When God is a Traveller*, and an anthology of sacred verse, *Eating God: A Book of Bhakti Poetry*.

Aryaman Khandelwal

Aryaman is a Dubai-based student-athlete, currently studying in the eleventh grade, and writes an active philosophy blog: aryamankhandelwall.wordpress.com. He plays semi-professional football, but is keen on pursuing both football and writing as possible career paths.

Avantika Agarwal
Educator-turned-illustrator. Mother to a precocious pre-schooler. Fauji wife. Collector of trunks and Tupperware. Addicted to chai and clinically obsessed with stationery.

Bijal Vachharajani
When Bijal Vachharajani is not reading *Harry Potter*, she can be found traipsing around the jungles of India or baking with chocolate. In her spare time, she works as a consultant editor and writes about sustainable development so she can fund those trips and buy those expensive books. Bijal has a master's degree in Environment Security and Peace from Costa Rica. She is the author of two children's books, *So You Want to Know About the Environment* and *What's Neema Eating Today*?

Arathi Menon
Arathi Menon cannot sing, cook, sew or salsa but she did write *Leaving Home with Half a Fridge*, a memoir published by Pan Macmillan. She likes dragonflies, cats, dogs, books, travel and her grandma and tweets about none of them. By the way, @unopenedbottle is her twitter handle.

Helen D'souza
Helen D'souza is our only grandparent author here. The stories from her past wove their magic into bedtime tales for her young grandsons. She had a lifetime of storytelling, first as a kindergarten teacher and piano teacher in Jamshedpur, and then as a primary school principal. This story, told to her author daughter, Jane D'souza, is her last story, as she passed away soon after its telling.

Jerry Pinto

Jerry Pinto lives and works in Mumbai. He reads lots of books and likes going for walks and patting stray dogs on their rough heads.

Maegan Dobson Sippy

Maegan Dobson Sippy was born in Dubai. She traces her roots back to Yorkshire, but grew up on the east coast of the UK. She now lives in Bangalore with her husband, daughter, mother-in-law and cat, and spends her time reading children's picture books, and working as a freelance writer and editor.

Pranita Kocharekar

Pranita Kocharekar is an illustrator based in Mumbai. She engages herself with animals and spends a large amount of time gazing at the moon, stars and the sea. You can find her drawings at www.instagram.com/pranitart.

Saee Koranne-Khandekar

Saee Koranne-Khandekar is a food writer and consultant based in Mumbai. She is also the author of *Crumbs!*, a book on bread traditions.

Sejal Mehta

Sejal Mehta is a writer, editor and content consultant. An old travel hack, she has worked with *Lonely Planet Magazine India, National Geographic Traveller, Saevus Wildlife, Femina* and JPMorgan and written for publications including *Mint, BBC Top Gear, BBC Knowledge, DNA, The Free Press Journal* and *The Hindustan Times,* across genres. A fierce protector of the wild, with a self-confessed bias for big cats, she is the editor-in-chief at Nature InFocus. She tweets and posts on Instagram and Twitter as @snaggletooth_00.

Sreedevi Gopakumar

Sreedevi Gopakumar has been a copywriter, news anchor and voiceover artist, among others things. She now spends her time cooking up stories for children. She lives in Gurgaon with her husband, five-year-old son and puppy.

Vidya Balachander

Vidya Balachander is a freelance journalist currently based in Colombo, Sri Lanka. Formerly the features editor of *BBC Good Food*'s India edition, based in Mumbai, her writing has appeared in publications such as *NPR's The Salt, Roads & Kingdoms, National Geographic Traveller, Indian Express, Mint Lounge, Harper's Bazaar India, The City Story* and others.

Zainab Sulaiman

Zainab Sulaiman is a special educator with over five years of experience in teaching and raising funds in the non-profit sector. She enjoys writing fiction and hanging out with people far wiser than herself, namely, her children.

ABOUT THE EDITOR

Lalita Iyer writes for little people and big people and the little people in big people. She is the author of *I'm Pregnant, Not Terminally Ill, You Idiot!* (Amaryllis), *The Boy who Swallowed a Nail and Other Stories* (Scholastic) and *The Whole Shebang* (Bloomsbury). She has also contributed to two anthologies: *A Book of Light* (Speaking Tiger) and *Gifts of Teaching* (Scholastic). You can tweet to her @Lalitude.